THE GREAT CHOCOPLOT

CHRIS CALLAGHAN

ILLUSTRATED BY LALALIMOLA

Chicken House

2 PALMER STREET, FROME, SOMERSET BA11 1DS

Text © Chris Callaghan 2016
Illustrations © Lalalimola (Sandra Navarro) 2016

First published in Great Britain in 2016
Chicken House
2 Palmer Street
Frome, Somerset BA11 1DS
United Kingdom
www.chickenhousebooks.com

Cover and interior design by Steve Wells
Cover and interior illustrations by Lalalimola (Sandra Navarro)
Typeset by Dorchester Typesetting Group Ltd
Printed and bound in Great Britain by CPI Group (UK) Ltd,
Croydon CR0 4YY

The paper used in this Chicken House book is made from wood
grown in sustainable forests.

7 9 10 8

British Library Cataloguing in Publication data available.

ISBN 978-1-910002-51-3
eISBN 978-1-910655-57-3

For Trinity
(to make you smile)

WARNING!

THIS STORY CONTAINS A THREAT

TO CHOCOLATE WHICH SOME

READERS MAY FIND DISTURBING.

CHAPTER 1

'In six days there will be no more chocolate in the world ... ever!'

That's what it said on *The Seven Show*.

Jelly had nearly reached the next level of Zombie Puppy Dash, but hearing this made her plunge the pink puppy into a huge tank of zombie dog food.

'Woah! What was that about chocolate?' she asked, putting her tablet down.

'Something about it running out,' said Mum, popping a chunk of chocolate into her mouth. 'Oh, you can't beat a Blocka Choca, eh!'

Jelly and her mum and dad loved Blocka Chocas.

Who didn't? Once a week Mum bought one bar for each of them, and they all curled up on the sofa together to enjoy them before Mum started her night shift at the supermarket.

'Chocolate's always mysteriously running out in this house,' said Dad, who'd already finished his Blocka Choca and was now eating cheese and onion crisps. 'I'm sure there was a Chunky Choc-Chip Crispie in the cupboard yesterday, but today it has vanished!'

'I don't know why you're looking at me,' Mum said, poking him in the belly, which was stretching the buttons of his checked shirt to their limit.

'Oh, that's right, blame me.'

'I do.'

'Good!'

'Good!'

'Ssh!' said Jelly. 'I'm trying to listen!'

The Seven Show's chirpy and very tanned presenter Alice was saying, 'And now over to our man in the jungle and the scary chocolate prophecy!'

The screen cut to a lush green tropical paradise, like Jelly had seen on documentaries about endangered species, or advertising a holiday her parents could never afford.

The caption on the screen read 'Easter Egg Island', and the reporter was a man called Martin who had a wonky but fake-looking smile which always made Jelly lick her front teeth and wonder if hers were as white and shiny. He did the silly bits on the show, like the old steam train found buried on a beach in Wales and the dog that fell in love with an owl. Today he was standing next to an old man with wild, grey hair that stuck up in patches.

Behind them was what looked like a huge stone

egg, twice the height of Jelly's dad and covered in jungle vines. It looked like it had been sprayed with green party streamers.

'Thank you, Alice,' said Martin. 'I'm here on Easter Egg Island. This is the little island in the middle of the Atlantic Ocean – *not* Easter Island in the Pacific, folks.' He chuckled. 'Here with me is chocolate expert Professor Fizziwicks from the University of Shambridge. He is convinced that he has

discovered a prophecy by the ancient civilization which once lived here and, if you can believe it, worshipped chocolate!'

The camera zoomed in to the egg-shaped stone. It was covered with weird-looking marks and scratches.

'Yes, indeed!' said the professor, who spoke like his tongue was too big for his mouth. Jelly could see it was lolling out like a thirsty dog's, and he was spraying spit everywhere!

'Ew!' said Jelly, wrinkling her nose.

'The ancient Chocolati tribe who lived on this island over a thousand years ago created this egg, and others like it scattered throughout, as part of their worship, and it is believed,' he chuckled, 'that if you break one open, you'll find a tiny bag of chocolate buttons inside!'

'Cool!' said Jelly.

'However, more importantly, these markings here and here' – Professor Fizziwicks pointed at the egg – 'clearly indicate that during the sixty-sixth cycle of Cacao-Cacao, which refers of course to the movement of the stars on the Summer Solstice, there will be a—' He paused and Martin the reporter wiped the spit from his face with a tissue before leaning in.

'A ... what?'

'A cataclysmic cacao catastrophe!' the professor spat. 'A Chocopocalypse!'

'A choco-what?' Martin asked, his face shining with fresh saliva.

'A Chocopocalypse!' grinned the professor. 'This amazing stone predicts the total and complete disintegration of cocoa products at a precise predetermined point in time—'

'You what?'

The professor sighed. 'It means that on the Summer Solstice – the twenty-first of June, this very Sunday – chocolate will simply cease to exist. A Chocopocalypse means what it means – a chocolate apocalypse. It's the end of chocolate!'

Jelly, her mum and her dad looked at each other with open mouths.

'That's mad!' Jelly said.

'It also predicts,' continued the professor, pointing to more scratches on the egg stone, 'that during the countdown to the catastrophe, a shower of chocolate shall rain down upon Easter Egg Island.'

Martin the reporter turned to face the camera with his wonky smile. 'A shower of chocolate,' he chuckled. 'I'd like to see that. Anyway, there you have it. The Chocopocalypse is coming! And on that bombshell, back to the studio to find out why dogs dream and cats don't ...'

'Well it wouldn't affect us here in Chompton anyway,' said Dad, switching off the TV. 'There's more chocolate shops here than there are people.'

It was true – their town of Chompton-on-de-Lyte was famous for being the world's biggest chocolate centre. They had more chocolate shops, factories and warehouses than any other country. And even though Dad and lots of his friends had recently lost their jobs at the Big Choc Lot because of 'cutbacks' (though nobody knew what that really meant), it was still the largest chocolate warehouse on earth. Enormous (but not pretty) ships came in and out of the river port, loading and unloading chocolate cargoes.

Local Chompton legend told that in 1522, the intrepid explorer Sir Walter Waffle returned from an epic expedition with Britain's first shipload of chocolate. But instead of sailing down the Thames to London to unveil his new treats to King Henry VIII (who had an extremely sweet tooth), he lost his bearings and ended up on the River de Lyte instead. Chompton had been at the centre of the chocolate world ever since.

Jelly stretched out on the sofa, her legs across her mum and dad's. 'But how could chocolate just run out?' she said. 'I mean, chocolate comes from ... plants. Doesn't it?'

She flicked open her tablet again and typed: 'What is chocolate?'

'Chocolate is derived from cacao beans, more commonly known as cocoa beans, from pods on the cacao tree,' she read out. She knew her mum and dad loved to listen to her read, and she often read to them in bed to help them go to sleep. 'The Mayan and Aztec civilizations drank a form of chocolate known as *Theobrama Cacao* – meaning "Food of the Gods" – centuries before it was shipped to Europe and developed into solid bars.'

'So even if the cacao tree did die out,' Mum said, 'there would still be tonnes of chocolate left in the world.'

'Yeah, and let's remember that was *The Seven Show* we were watching, not the Open University,' added Dad. 'Last week they said that eating lots of bacon will give you a sun tan. Well, when me and your mum were first married, I had a bacon buttie every day, and did I look like I lived in the Bahamas? No, I did not!'

'There's an app for it already!' Jelly said, still looking at her tablet.

'For what?' asked Dad, looking interested. 'Bacon butties?'

'No! The Chocopocalypse. "*The countdown to the end of chocolate*", it says here. It's free. Can I? Please?'

Dad nodded. 'All right then, give it here. I'll put the password in for you.'

'I already know the password,' said Jelly, feeling insulted. 'I'm not a baby.'

But once the app had downloaded, Jelly suddenly didn't want to look at it. She slid the tablet back down the side of the sofa and tried to forget about the Chocopocalypse.

She was always being told (usually by her mum) to stop worrying. But it wasn't as simple as that. You can't stop worrying about something just because someone tells you to stop worrying. Even if you want to stop, it doesn't mean you can. To be told that she was always worrying made her think she did worry too much, and this worried her even more.

Could the world really run out of chocolate?

Jelly was worried!

COUNTDOWN TO THE CHOCOPOCALYPSE:

5 DAYS, 11 HOURS, 24 MINUTES, 23 SECONDS

CHOCOPOCAL-APP NEWS

No one knows what happened to the Ancient Easter Egg Islanders. One theory is that is that they all left the island in search of Chocolate Paradise. Another is that they became extinct after eating too much chocolate. Professor Fizziwicks of the University of Shambridge believes they were abducted by aliens.

CHAPTER 2

After helping her mum tie her long brown hair back into a tight ponytail with various hairbands and clips, Jelly kissed her goodnight and off her mum went to start another twelve-hour night shift at the twenty-four-hour supermarket. Jelly left her dad attempting to repair a rip in one of Mum's skirts with a needle and thread (she hated the sight of blood, and with her dad in charge of a needle there was guaranteed to be some) and went up to her bedroom. Sitting in her comfy reclining chair with her feet up on her bed, she stared up at the giant mosaic of her mum and dad she'd made out of old chocolate wrappers, and pondered.

It was crazy, and Jelly knew it, but she couldn't stop thinking about the Chocopocalypse. What if the world *did* run out of chocolate? Did that include chocolate-flavoured things? And chocolate biscuits? And chocolate ice cream?

Why did she love chocolate so much anyway? She couldn't find the words. Maybe the proper words didn't exist. Chocolate had a kind of ... sort of ... meltilicious chocodreaminess about it. She loved it more than chips or pizza. Even more than doughnuts or strawberry laces.

Did she love it more than her mum and dad? *No, that's not fair*, she thought. It was completely different. (Wasn't it?)

And why was a little chunk of chocolate never enough? Did they put something in it to make you always want another one? It was the same with peanuts and mobile phones and ...

Now she was thinking about Blocka Choca bars again!

She wondered if there was any more chocolate downstairs. Sometimes there was an Ice Choc hidden in the freezer behind the frozen broccoli or runner beans. It was always a good surprise to find one, like some hidden gem, when she helped make the tea. But no – she'd been in the freezer yesterday and there wasn't even any frozen broccoli to hide behind.

Mum and Dad always left the shopping until Mum's monthly payday, by which time there would be absolutely nothing left in the fridge, the freezer or any cupboard. When they did do the shopping, the Wellington family would eat like spoilt celebrities for a week, and then things got back to normal – like having a fish finger and a sausage with some pasta for tea.

'Make-do' meals was what Mum called them.

'Surprise-specials' was what Dad said.

'Bad-parenting' was what Gran grumbled.

Gran, Jelly suddenly thought. She'd definitely have chocolate.

Gran lived in an old caravan on the drive. The Gran-a-van, they called it.

Their next-door neighbour, Mrs Bunstable, was always complaining; in her opinion, it blocked her view. In Jelly's opinion, the only view it blocked was the grey portakabin on the pavement that measured traffic pollution on their street, Waffle Way West.

But Mrs Bunstable just liked to know everyone else's business – and then talk about it to all her old lady friends.

Gran had lived in the Gran-a-van for about a year now, since Grandad had died. There wasn't enough room for her in their small stone terraced house, which had been built nearly one hundred years ago to house the workers at the port, and the caravan was all they had been able to afford. It was a really old pumpkin-shaped one with a date on its side showing it was even older than Dad, and it was

covered in a patchwork of repairs and rust-coloured stains (just like Dad). Still, Gran loved it. She said it was like being on an adventure, and that one day the Gran-a-van would magically turn into a golden coach and whisk her off to a fancy ball.

Jelly rapped on the caravan door.

'Friend or foe?' came a voice from inside.

'Granddaughter!' giggled Jelly.

After a few moments, the door opened and Gran's wide grin greeted her, along with a waft of the caravan's musty smell.

'Friend, definitely a friend,' she said, taking her headphones from around her neck.

You could always hear the motorway noise through the thin metal walls of the Gran-a-van, and so Gran wore her trusty headphones most of the time, even though they made her look like some kind of OAP rapper.

'Come in, Jennifer dear, come in.'

Gran was one of the few people who called Jelly by her real name. When she was a baby, her parents had called her 'Jelly Welly' (because their surname was Wellington) and the name had stuck. She didn't particularly mind being called Jelly – there were certainly worse things to be called (like Smelly Jelly Welly when she was a toddler!) and she had got used to it. At least she wasn't called William like her dad – having a childhood nickname of 'Willy Welly' explained a lot about his behaviour.

'Did you see that funny thing on the telly about the world running out of chocolate?' asked Jelly, moving a book from the worn sofa bed so she could sit down.

'No dear, I've been reading. In between snoozes.' Gran straightened her bright yellow woollen cardigan, which always looked like it had shrunk in the wash, and settled her small, plump body next to Jelly. She fitted in quite well with all the badly stuffed cushions around her.

'There was this really weird professor saying that on Sunday there will be no chocolate left.'

'Oh, my stars!' laughed Gran, making her plastic-framed glasses slide to the end of her nose. 'Well, in that case' – she opened a drawer next to her – 'take your pick, dear, before they all disappear!'

Jelly chose a Blocka Choca bar from Gran's special chocolate drawer, which was looking unusually empty, feeling a little guilty that this had been her real reason for calling in.

Gran continued rummaging around. 'Oh dear, none of my ginger chocolate left. Never mind, I'll have a Blocka Choca too.'

'What are you reading, Gran?' Jelly asked as they chomped away. She turned the pages of the book next to her. It looked very weighty and serious, bound in tatty red leather, without even a picture on the front.

'Oh, that old thing?' Gran said. 'It's nothing. I'm just being nostalgic and silly.'

'*The Philosophical Transgressions in Science: Compendium 1964*,' read Jelly, struggling with the long words. She opened it at the contents page and skimmed through some of the chapter titles: *Silly String Theory*, *A Brief History of Slime*, *A General Theory of Especially Annoying Relatives* ...

Then she spotted a familiar name. '*The Positive in the Negative* by A. T. Curtin.' She looked at Gran. 'That's you!'

Curtin was her gran's maiden name, and Jelly had known she'd worked in a laboratory when she was younger, but had never asked her about it.

'You've had your work published in a book?' Jelly asked now, surprised.

'Oh, just bits and pieces, dear,' said Gran, her cheeks growing pink. 'Nonsense, really. That was the last thing I had published before your mum was born. Well, the last thing I ever had published, in fact. Gave it all up, of course.' She settled herself against the cushions. 'Back then it was a woman's job to bring up the children and I did it gladly.'

Jelly nodded. She had heard all the stories of her grandad being the worst bus driver in the world, so it seemed a shame that Gran had had to stop her work instead. But Jelly missed him hugely. Her favourite memories of him were Sunday afternoon visits, when after a roast dinner and few bottles of chocolate stout he'd launch into a country and western sing-a-long. She wished she could listen to him singing 'A Cowgirl Stole My Horse' just one more time.

'What kind of things did you do in your lab?' asked Jelly, breaking off another chunk of Blocka Choca.

Gran smiled and gently ran her finger across her printed name. For just a moment, she looked different somehow – whether it was pride or sadness, Jelly couldn't quite tell.

'I was part of a team in London. Our research centre was just around the corner from Downing Street, you know.'

'Really?' asked Jelly. 'That close?' She had just done a school topic on Number 10 Downing Street, where the Prime Minister lived.

'Oh yes,' replied Gran. 'I could see the PM's front door from the room where I worked.' She hesitated. 'Well, you could see it from the ladies' toilet ... if you stood on a chair!'

'So what did you do there?' said Jelly, leaning

forward.

'We carried out research and experiments to confirm that something didn't work.'

'That something *didn't* work?' asked Jelly, confused.

Gran laughed. 'I suppose it sounds quite loony when you say it out loud! But sometimes that's science for you.'

It didn't make complete sense, but Jelly quite liked the fact that she didn't fully understand it, and she looked at her gran with new-found admiration. Gran had been a real scientist, doing mad science things!

'Can I read it?' Jelly said, straightening the book's dog-eared pages and battered corners.

Gran shrugged. 'If you like. Not that it's good bedtime reading,' she added with a laugh. 'It's so boring it'll probably send you right off to sleep.'

A little while later, Jelly found out that it did exactly that!

CHAPTER 3

Sharp sunlight filled her bedroom as Jelly peeled the curtains back and opened the window. A lovely cool breeze was accompanied by the usual dawn chorus of lorries, cars and motorbikes.

The M891 motorway passed right by her house, just at the end of the back garden. Lorries and vans delivering chocolate were a constant part of life in Chompton.

Jelly actually liked all the traffic; it made her feel like she was at the centre of the chocolate world. Every morning she would watch the snail-like progress of the pollution-pumping vehicles and give the drivers a wave. Once in a while she'd get a wave back. It always amazed her what people did while driving their slow-moving vehicles: shaving, eating, putting on make-up and even reading books!

She waved to a lorry driver who was picking his nose, and got ready for school.

Half an hour later, Jelly was in the back garden, munching on toast and wondering whether to wear a cardigan. As usual, she had tied her long brown hair in a high ponytail, just like Mum. She loved the way it swayed about her head and she strode about the garden purposefully to encourage its swooshing motion.

'What are you doing at school today?' Dad shouted above the din of the traffic.

Jelly shrugged. 'Same as usual, probably,' she yelled back, and watched as Dad proudly watered the large clump of weeds in the corner of the garden. Nobody had the heart to explain to him that they weren't actually flowers. Nothing proper ever grew in their garden, probably because of all the pollution from the motorway.

Switching the hose off, Dad stood back to admire

the mass of tangled stems and leaves with the odd small yellow bud poking out.

'They're coming on nicely, aren't they?' he bellowed.

'Yeah,' Jelly called back. 'They're ... lovely. What are *you* doing today, Dad?'

'Dave said he might have a job for me,' Dad said, and Jelly made a face.

She didn't like Dave much – her mum called him 'Dodgy Dave' – but Dad sometimes did some work for him, like removing old kitchens or unloading lorries or fitting electrics. Dad always promised he would never do anything 'dodgy', and Jelly believed him, but she was still worried that since he'd lost his job at the Big Choc Lot he might be tempted.

Putting it from her mind, Jelly decided it was a no-cardie-day. She waved goodbye to Dad and grabbed her school bag, swinging it in wide circles as she left the house.

Mr Walker, who lived two doors down, on the other side of Mrs Bunstable, was standing on the grass verge with his little Yorkshire terrier squatting beside him.

'How is Truffles today?' asked Jelly, already

knowing the answer.

'It's been three days now,' said Mr Walker frowning, 'and we haven't used a single poo bag. We can't get his usual doggy chocs anywhere. They used to keep him regular!'

Jelly looked at the straining Truffles and felt sorry for him. That had to be uncomfortable. 'I'm sure he'll be OK soon,' she said.

She would usually give Truffles a gentle rub on the head, but decided not to today. She wouldn't like someone rubbing her head while she tried to have a poo.

Every morning, on her way to school, Jelly would walk down Cookie Way, and past the old softplay Barmy Bounce on Bittersweet Street. She used to go there when she was little and had especially loved the ball pit and the holes in the mesh that weren't meant to be there – she'd always had brilliant fun confusing, and sometimes scaring, Mum and Dad by disappearing from the ball pit and turning up somewhere completely different.

Sadly it had been closed by the council after Dad

and Dodgy Dave had installed an Emergency Off Button to shut down all the electrics when needed. Dave's dodgy wiring had caused the slushy machines to overheat and the dodgems to go too fast! Someone's dad had got stuck between two dodgem cars without anybody noticing – until a group of Brownies pulled him free. He had sued Barmy Bounce for unlawful imprisonment, and the Brownies for assault.

On the corner of Cookie Way and Bittersweet Street was a large bronze statue of Sir Walter Waffle holding out a block of chocolate. It used to be considered lucky to lick the block, but there was now a Hygiene Regulation sign (with a warning of a hefty fine) that said 'No Licking'.

The shop on the corner itself was Chompton-on-de-Lyte's newest, trendiest and most expensive chocolate shop: Chox. It never seemed to have customers. Jelly wasn't surprised – why would anyone pay high prices for posh Chox chocolate, when there were dozens of cheap chocolate shops just down the road?

It was so posh and pricey that Jelly had never dared go in before. But it was Gran's birthday next week, and she wanted to get her some really special ginger chocolate in a nice box for her special chocolate drawer. She stared into the shop window. Fairy lights and candles illuminated the display, and shining fabrics had been draped luxuriously around glittering purple and brown boxes. Some were open, displaying tiny, delicate dollops of dark chocolate. A sign, which had not been there yesterday, was stretched across the window:

'**THE END OF CHOCOLATE IS UPON YOU!**'

Just underneath it said 'No Children', but Jelly thought the owner couldn't mean that. No children in a chocolate shop? Maybe it was a joke ...

She took a deep breath and pushed the door open. It buzzed loudly which sounded as if someone was being electrocuted, and Jelly jumped, then felt a bit embarrassed.

The first thing she noticed was how cold and unwelcoming the shop was. And it smelt somehow a little bit rotten. It reminded her of the teachers' staff room and made her shiver.

Just as she was pondering whether to stay, from behind a towering display of purple chocolate boxes a man at least as old as her gran popped up. He had dark-brown hair that flopped over his face, an elaborate moustache and a long pointed nose. He glowered at Jelly through narrow eyes.

'The sign says "no children",' he snapped.

Jelly could not make out his accent. It wasn't quite French or Spanish or Dutch, but then it wasn't quite right for anything – almost like a combination of every language that existed. Jelly suspected he was putting it on.

'I'm s-orry ... but I'm only h-here because ... I'd like some ... some ch-chocolate please,' she stammered nervously. 'It's f-for my gran.'

The man sighed impatiently. 'Well, obviously you're here to buy chocolate,' he hissed. 'This is a chocolate shop.'

'Yes ... obviously ...' Jelly said awkwardly. 'But what I wanted was ... ginger chocolate.'

'*Ginger chocolate?*' he spat, raising his thick eyebrows impossibly high.

As he stepped out from behind the large display, Jelly was surprised to see him wearing some sort of brown safari suit – the kind people wore on documentaries about endangered animals. It looked exactly like it had been made out of Gran's caravan curtains. In his hands were a cup and saucer, and one of his little fingers was sticking out at a perfect right angle (which was how Mum drank her coffee whenever they visited posh Auntie Agatha). Jelly breathed in the distinctive aroma of hot chocolate, but it smelt a bit strong – bitter almost, and she could see that the colour of it was almost black.

'I am Gari – Garibaldi Chocolati – and I sell only the finest chocolate known to the human race!' he

exclaimed. 'The finest and the *purest*. I take the greatest care to find premium quality products from original sources.'

He put down his cup, and pointed to a wall full of framed photos of himself in various exotic locations. In each, he was wearing the same immaculate brown safari suit and inspecting sacks full of beans or fields of cacao trees.

'I offer not just the best chocolate in this town, but the best chocolate in the world,' he went on, 'and you want *ginger chocolate*!'

'Um – yes, please,' answered Jelly, suddenly wishing she'd gone to get it somewhere else.

'You'll be asking for one of those hideous Blocka Choca bars next!' he went on.

'Yes, I'll have one of those too, please,' said Jelly, starting to get annoyed with this very rude man.

Gari had just picked his cup up again but slammed it back down and disappeared behind the counter, tutting and sighing dramatically.

As she waited Jelly heard a crashing noise down a long corridor behind him. At the far end, she was sure she could see the ball pits and brightly coloured walls of the old Barmy Bounce. It made sense, she supposed, working out that the play area must be at the back of Chox. She could just make someone out in the distant gloom who seemed to be moving large boxes about (and maybe dropping a few). He seemed to be talking on the phone (so no wonder he was dropping things).

Gari rummaged, tutted and sighed some more, until finally he dropped a tiny purple box on to the counter. The word 'Chox' was written in swirly letters across it.

'*The only chocolate worth buying*,' he purred, and flipped open the lid with a flourish, flicking his dark hair to one side as he did so.

Jelly was hit by an invisible cloud of pungent, bitter chocolate. Her knees quivered and suddenly she felt as if she might faint.

'You may try a small sample,' said Gari, holding out the teeniest piece of almost-black chocolate on a cocktail stick.

Jelly took the stick and cautiously put the chocolate into her mouth. It was awful!

'It meets with your approval, yes?' asked the shopkeeper, arching an eyebrow.

'Erm ... well,' said Jelly, trying to breathe through her mouth and not her nose, and not to spit out the horrible chocolate.

Closing the box, he snapped, 'That'll be twenty pounds.'

'What?' blurted out Jelly. 'Twenty pounds, for that tiny box?'

He shrugged his shoulders. 'Prices have gone up.' He pointed to the sign in the window. 'Because of the Chocopocalypse.'

Jelly held open her wallet and peered inside. All she had was twenty pounds, which had taken her ages to save up especially for Gran's birthday. She was planning on getting the chocolate and a few other things for Gran. She didn't like this posh Chox chocolate, but maybe Gran would ...

Feeling worried, she was about to hand Gari the twenty-pound note when she noticed a small white insect scuttle across the counter. It looked a bit like a woodlouse, or the flying ants that were sometimes in their garden on really hot days.

'Er, no thanks,' she said, backing away from the counter. 'I'll leave it for today.'

She didn't wait to hear what Gari said.

The buzz of the door sounded as Jelly scuttled from the shop, making her jump again, but she felt relieved to be out of that horrible place.

Insects in a chocolate shop? she thought as she ran on to school. Yuck!

CHAPTER 4

'Did you see that nutter on *The Seven Show* last night?' asked Potsy Potter from the table behind Jelly. 'He was saying that there's going to be no more chocolate by Sunday. That's scary!'

'But you don't actually believe it, do you?' asked Jelly, turning round.

They were in the classroom, waiting for their teacher, Mr Tatterly, to arrive for registration.

'Course I don't,' he said, going red, 'I'm not an idiot. I'm just saying – what a nutter!'

'You watch *The Seven Show*?' Maya, Jelly's best friend, asked with a smile. 'I mean, are you like a hundred or something?'

'Me mum and dad watch it,' he replied defensively. 'It was just on. I wasn't properly watching.'

Both Jelly and Maya turned back round, grinning.

'But did you see it, Jell?' whispered Maya. 'That professor bloke was officially creepy – and imagine if it was true. I mean, I know it isn't true. But just imagine if it was!' Her mouth dropped open. 'It'd be a proper nightmare.'

'So do *you* watch *The Seven Show*?' asked Jelly, with a twinkle in her eye.

'Well, it's just on in the background – you know what I mean!'

'Yeah,' said Jelly. 'I know what you mean.'

Mr Tatterly fell into the classroom, books from his arms spilling out on to the floor. He tried desperately to hold on to some remaining books, tuck his shirt in and stop his glasses falling off – but failed miserably at all three.

'I'll manage,' he said to no one in particular.

He picked the books up and settled them into a pile on his desk, only for them to all slowly slide off, back on to the floor.

'I hope everyone is getting on well with their science experiment video,' he said, collecting the books up again and trying to find his glasses.

Most of the class nodded, which made Jelly's heart beat with alarm. She hadn't even started yet, and she didn't have a clue what to do it about. It had been worrying her for ages, and because she had been worrying about it, she hadn't started it. And because she hadn't started it, she had worried about it even more. It was the eternal cycle of worry.

'Remember,' continued Mr Tatterly, picking up the last few books, 'it's about the scientific process, more than the content. It can be about anything at

all. But it must include the four elements of … ?'

The class replied with a familiar silence.

'The four elements of: question, experiment, results and conclusion,' he answered for them with a sigh. 'I want you all to upload your videos on to the school's website, look at everyone else's and click the "like" button on the video that you think explains the whole process the best. The deadline is this Sunday night, when I'll check the videos and count the "likes".'

Jelly's heart sank. If she didn't get enough 'likes' she might be moved down a group and end up with Dante Durden, who spent all day picking scabs off his knuckles. She had already been warned about 'lack of focus' on her school report. But how could she focus when she worried too much about getting everything right? It wasn't as if she couldn't do the work – she just couldn't do the work *in time*. Sometimes the lessons seemed to disappear before she'd got going.

'What's the prize for the winner, Mr Tatterly?' asked Potsy Potter, munching loudly.

'Are you … eating … chocolate, Potter?' Mr Tatterly tried to bellow, though his voice was only slightly more frightening than a meerkat.

'Er, yes, sir,' grinned Potsy, who wasn't scared of Mr Tatterly. (Actually, nobody was.) 'It's a Whopper bar. I'm eating it now in case there aren't any left next week. I can sell you one if you like?'

'That's very kind of you, Potter,' said Mr Tatterly, looking tempted. 'But you and I both know that no one is allowed to eat food in school.'

'Not even at lunchtime?' came a voice from the back.

'Well ... obviously at lunchtime ... yes, but not during lessons is what I mean, and I think you all know that!'

'But we've got to make the most of the chocolate, before it all disappears,' said a freckle-faced girl called Louise, who also had chocolate all round her mouth.

'Ah yes,' laughed Mr Tatterly. 'The Chocopocalypse. I saw that last night on the television. I mean ... I didn't actually see it myself, but my wife told me.'

A whisper filled the classroom: 'He's got a wife! He's got a wife?'

'Yes ...' Mr Tatterly's cheeks flushed beetroot. 'I

do have a wife ... and she is rather pretty too.'

All the class looked at him with faces that clearly said, 'I don't think so!'

Jelly made her way home slowly after school. Her shoulders dropped as she saw Mrs Bunstable – or Mrs Bum-stubble, as Dad called her – standing outside the rusty gate she shared with the Wellingtons. Her black, wiry hair was held firmly in position with enough old-fashioned curlers for two bad hairstyles, let alone one, and as usual she was just nosing around and waiting for someone to talk at.

Mrs Bunstable had various tactics to trap innocent victims so she could gossip at them for as long as possible. She kept a tin of beans in her apron pocket, for example. The tin would be 'accidentally' dropped as a victim approached. She would reach down and let out an 'ooohhh ahhhh' while rubbing her back. The kind-hearted victim would be compelled to pick the tin up for her – and then she had them! The innocent fool would be left holding the tin out, but of course Mrs Bunstable would not take the tin. To take the tin would only allow the poor wretch to run for freedom. As long as she ignored the existence of the tin, she had all the power. She'd seen men grow beards while holding that tin.

It was impossible to avoid her – and Jelly had certainly tried! 'Hello, Mrs Bunstable,' she said quickly as she sprinted past her and up the path. She knew that even one word would be fatal – Mrs Bunstable would leap on it, manage somehow to twist it into some kind of gossip or even a personal attack and gleefully take it to her next Knit and Natter meeting, delighted to have something to gossip or complain about with all her old lady friends.

'My, you're growing up there fast, young Jennifer!' called Mrs Bunstable.

Why did grown-ups say things like that? Jelly was never sure what to say in return. A 'thank you' didn't seem to fit, and 'I'm a kid, that's what we do' seemed a bit rude.

'Yeah,' said Jelly. 'Too fast!' Which was something Mum would say.

'Haven't seen you for a while, treasure,' Mrs Bunstable called after her. 'I've a hospital appointment next week, you know!'

Jelly glanced over her shoulder as she opened the

front door, trying to look interested.

'It's my bladder again,' the old lady boomed. 'I've had to wait six weeks for my operation. Six weeks! It's a disgrace. But you know me, treasure, I don't like to complain.'

Jelly tried to close the door and nod sympathetically at the same time.

'Is your dad still lazing about the house, eh? It's all right for some,' Mrs Bunstable yelled, sounding now like Minnie Mouse shouting through a megaphone.

Jelly nodded quickly and shut the door with a sigh of relief – then listened to Mrs Bunstable slam her door (she *always* slammed it!) – and threw herself on the sofa to watch TV. After a little while, she thought she had better tidy up a bit before Mum came down. Once a few random cups and sweaty socks were picked up (Dad was such a scruff!) she almost opened the curtains at the back of their living room, but saw the figure of Mrs Bunstable loitering in their back garden, and decided to keep them closed. Their neighbour had a habit of squeezing through a gap in the fence (which Dad kept meaning to repair) and peering in on them through the windows, tapping on the glass if spot-ted. She would always pretend she had something important to tell them, but they all knew the real reason! She was on the trail for gossip!

A while later, Mum came downstairs dressed for work and yawning like a foghorn. Jelly couldn't re-member what Mum looked like when she wasn't yawning.

'Shift up, munchkin,' she said, and plonked her-self down with a groan.

Dad came in from the kitchen, carrying a bowl of porridge and a coffee.

'Breakfast is served, m'lady,' he said with a flourish of a tea towel, which he placed over Mum's lap to protect her smart work clothes from any stray dollops of por-ridge.

'Just once,' said Mum. 'Just once, I'd like to wake up to a sound which isn't that pain-in-the-bum woman. Why does she always have to slam her front door?'

'Tell me about it,' said Dad. 'I'm the one who has to listen when her cronies come round for tea and cake and they all get to gossiping together. And as for all the rubbish telly that she watches on full volume in the evening, while you're lucky enough to be at work!'

Mum shot him a fierce look.

'What're we having for tea, Dad?' asked Jelly, trying to change the subject.

'Well,' said Dad, taking a deep breath, 'it was supposed to be those crispy chicken things with chips, but we don't have any of those chicken things left. But we do have some ravioli.'

'Ravioli and chips sounds good to me.'

'But we don't have any chips left either,' said Dad with a frown. 'It's Mum's payday next week. I'll do some shopping then. Promise.'

'Is there anything else?' enquired Jelly, already knowing the answer.

'Not really,' confirmed Dad.

'We're fine, then,' said Jelly, and Mum agreed.

Dad disappeared into the kitchen and Mum gave Jelly a nudge.

'I hope you're helping your dad out,' she whispered, leaning in close to her. 'I don't get to do as much as I should, so I'm expecting you to do my bit for me, OK?'

Jelly nodded. 'I promise, Mum. I do help.'

Mum gave her a wink. 'I know you do, munchkin.'

Over the last year, since Mum had started her new job as a Trainee Deputy Assistant Junior Manager, working nights at the supermarket, not getting home until after Jelly had left for school, then sleeping days at home, Jelly and her dad had become a good team together.

He washed the dishes, while she dried them and put them away.

She was in charge of folding the clothes after Dad had ironed them.

General cleaning and tidying up was a bit more random. Dusting was usually done by blowing and running a finger along random surfaces, rather than using a duster. Although Dad had become obsessed with the vacuuming lately – he'd spend ages trying to get lines on the living-room carpet, just like on a Wimbledon tennis court.

Before long Dad returned with two plates of ravioli on toast. On Jelly's plate there was a special treat of a cheese slice draped across the top, melting deliciously into the ravioli. Dad had once told her that this was something the very top restaurants did, but

Jelly wasn't sure if she believed him.

When they had finished tea, the theme tune to *The Seven Show* started. 'They might mention that chocolatey-apocalatey thing again,' said Dad.

'The Chocopocalypse?' corrected Jelly with a grin. 'Yeah, they might.' She really hoped they would. Maybe then she could stop worrying about it.

Dad reached for the remote and turned up the volume, and they all loudly sang along to the theme tune.

CHAPTER 5

Alice was on the screen. 'We now go live,' she announced, 'to Easter Egg Island. Where it has been predicted that chocolate will rain from the sky any day now. How's it looking there, Martin?' she chuckled. 'Have you got your umbrella up?'

The camera cut to a huge expanse of jungle, with a clear blue sky beautifully illuminating the now-familiar sight of the colossal egg-shaped rock monument.

'No sign of any rain yet,' laughed Martin, flashing his wonky smile and white teeth, 'but I can see a small cloud. That's quite a rare thing here. I think it looks a bit like a rabbit. Look, you can just make out its fluffy white tail.'

The camera focused on a small spindly cloud.

'I think it looks more like a train,' said Alice. 'You can see the smoke coming out.'

'No,' disagreed Martin. 'It's definitely a rabbit.'

'OK, thanks again, Martin,' laughed Alice. 'We'll be back for a final word before the end of the show.'

After a short film about a seagull being used to spy on the Nazis during the Second World War, and a piece about a man who had bumped his head and afterwards could only read books upside-down, Alice pressed her finger into her earpiece.

'Er ... I understand we now have a situation on Easter Egg Island,' she said, 'so it's over to you again, Martin.'

This time the TV screen became a green blur; the speakers making a strange, deep, gurgling noise.

Jelly, her mum and her dad all leant towards the screen.

'What's going on?' Mum said.

'I think the cameraman's running,' said Jelly, frowning.

Then came the sound of Martin breathing heavily,

before the image focused on his frantic face. 'Can you hear me, Alice? Are we on-air?' he panted.

'We can hear you, Martin,' called out Alice. 'Are you OK?'

'I'll have to assume you can hear me ... right ... We've had to move because the ground started shaking like mad ... rocks and stones from the summit above the ancient egg rock were falling ... a couple of huge boulders just missed us ... it got a bit "Indiana Jones" there for a minute.'

He seemed to gradually calm down, his eyes weren't quite as wide and jittery, and the camera stopped shaking.

'Well, that was exciting,' he laughed. 'That's live TV, folks!'

He stared into the distance suddenly, standing perfectly still. At first Jelly wasn't sure whether it was the TV that had frozen or Martin himself.

'Can you hear that?' he asked. 'That rumbling sound? Is there going to be another quake? I think there's going to be another quake!'

The rumbling became clearer and louder. The TV image shook. This time, it was clear that the cameraman was not running – it was the ground that was shaking!

'Look ... b-b-back at the stone egg ...' stuttered Martin. 'It's ... it's ...'

The camera swung round, revealing a shaky picture of the ancient monument. There seemed to be

something spurting out of holes all over it. Jets of dark fluid were shooting up into the air and spraying all around the jungle.

'It's ... it's ... *chocolate*!' shouted Martin over the roaring. '*It's raining chocolate!*'

Jelly, her mum and her dad stared at the TV.

'Woah,' gasped Jelly.

'I hope that Martin bloke packed an extra pair of shorts,' added Dad. 'He looks well freaked out!'

'You don't think ...' said Mum, grasping Jelly's hand for comfort, 'that it could be ... you know ... true?'

Jelly shook her head, but as the programme ended in confusion, she wasn't sure at all what to think.

Even the man introducing the next programme seemed surprised: 'Right ...' he stuttered. 'Well, next tonight we have ... er ... let's see ... where's my bit of paper ... ah yes ... we have "Cheese and Toilet Paper" ... oh no, sorry ... that's my shopping list—' A clip of the next *Doctor Who* episode flashed on to the screen, cutting him off.

To cheer them all up, Dad tried to make hot chocolate with some of the real cocoa beans he'd been given after losing his job at the Big Choc Lot. He bashed them with a hammer and boiled them up with milk. Unfortunately it just tasted like warm milk with bits in.

I bet Garibaldi Chocolati would know what to do with those beans, Jelly thought, as she brushed her teeth for ages to get rid of the cocoa bits.

But she'd never ask him – not in a million years.

'Did you just watch *The Seven Show*, Gran?' asked Jelly, climbing into the caravan later to help Gran charge her phone.

'Heavens to Betsy, I don't watch that tat,' Gran sniffed. 'I was reading.' She hurriedly rolled up what looked suspiciously like a celebrity gossip magazine and stuffed it under the cushion she was sitting on.

'It's just that there might be something in this Chocopocalypse thing after all,' Jelly said, as she looked around for Gran's phone charger.

She found it on the windowsill in a large bowl full of pens and receipts and Gran's headphones. Moving the curtain to one side, she looked out and caught a glimpse of Mr Walker on the grass verge with Truffles beside him. He was too far away for

Jelly to see how Truffles was doing, but the look on Mr Walker's face said that it was not going well!

The curtains reminded Jelly of the horrible man from Chox. It made her shudder. 'Why don't you get some new curtains, Gran?' she asked.

'What's the matter with my curtains?' Gran looked offended.

'Well, they're ... brown!'

'They're not brown, they are *butterscotch*,' Gran corrected.

Jelly plugged the phone into the charger, which finally gave a satisfying 'beep' after she had switched the socket on and off a few times.

'Has Dad been messing around with your electricity again?' she asked.

'He put some energy-saving bulbs in the other day and I've had to use this ever since.' Gran waved a torch around and rolled her eyes.

'Gran,' said Jelly, sitting back down, 'from a scientist's point of view, about this chocolate thing – what would be your ... conclusion?'

'Oh, I couldn't make a conclusion. I couldn't even make an assumption. There is no data. There is no evidence ...'

There was a sudden loud crashing noise just out-side the caravan, making them both jump.

Gran peeped behind the curtain. 'It's that woman! Putting her rubbish in our bin again. I don't know how she has the nerve.'

'But what about this "Positive in the Negative" stuff you used to do?' continued Jelly, frowning. 'Making conclusions out of things that don't hap-pen?'

'Hmmm, well yes, of course, you're right, smartie pants,' smiled Gran. She reached for a notepad and raked about in the windowsill bowl for a pen. 'Right, tell me exactly what you know.'

Gran scribbled furiously as Jelly ex-plained the Chocopocalypse. After Jelly had finished, Gran stared at the notepad for so long that Jelly wondered if she had fallen asleep. It wouldn't have been the first time – last week Gran had ended up at the bus depot after missing her stop on a visit to a friend. She had said that she had been 'concentrating on a thought too hard', but they all suspected she had been snoozing.

'OK!' Gran's sudden shout made Jelly jump. 'You would need to set up an *experiment*.' Her eyes twinkled under the battery-powered reading lamp. 'There is a very simple experiment that we can carry out to determine whether the Chocopocalypse is real or fake.'

'Really?' asked Jelly, her brain bursting with curiosity. 'What?'

'Get some chocolate ...' Gran rummaged around in her drawer. There was one Blocka Choca bar left. She held it out and Jelly took it solemnly.

'Yes.'

'Put it in a sealed container ...'

'Yes.'

'Put it somewhere safe and don't interfere with it ...'

'Yes.'

'Wait until Sunday ...'

'Yes.'

'And then open it. If there's no chocolate – the Chocopocalypse has happened. If the chocolate is still there – it hasn't!'

'Really?' said Jelly, frowning.

'Science isn't all about explosions and ... whizzy things, you know.'

Jelly sat back and pondered. Question, experiment,

results and conclusion – that was what Mr Tatterly had said. At least here was a question, and a really important one: was the Chocopocalypse real?

Now all she had to do was prove it.

COUNTDOWN TO THE CHOCOPOCALYPSE:

3 DAYS, 23 HOURS, 59 MINUTES, 02 SECONDS

CHOCOPOCAL-APP NEWS

A Chocopocalypse Crisis Helpline dealing with public concerns has been criticized for taking advantage of people by charging £2.50 per minute for calls. A further helpline has been set up for those wanting to complain about this. Calls cost £3.50 per minute.

The winners of today's British Formula 1 Grand Prix sprayed themselves with chocolate milkshake instead of champagne. Horrified onlookers heckled and booed the podium after seeing the extravagant waste. Later, the race winner Jemstone Bottom said, 'I'm so handsome, I can get away with anything.'

CHAPTER 6

Jelly loved being in the kitchen first thing in the morning when Mum was still at work and Dad was fast asleep. The sun shone directly into the kitchen for only a short time before it moved behind the motorway sign for Junction 43. As the traffic sped past behind the garden railings, light glinted through the collection of glasses on the draining board. All the colours of the rainbow, refracted from the glasses, flickered and danced about the kitchen walls. When Jelly squinted – and ignored the toaster held together with duct tape, and the fridge door being kept shut by a badly scorched ironing board, and the crusted remains of ravioli in a pan by the sink – she thought it was beautiful.

Standing on tiptoes she reached up to the cupboard where they kept things that didn't have a home anywhere else.

There were bits of an old barbecue, a box of screws, a mess of tangled leads, a sandwich maker and even one of Dad's old cocoa beans, which Jelly sniffed and then put into her pocket.

But right at the back of the cupboard was what she was looking for: a metal box. She had no idea what it had originally been used for, but its current job was to keep safe all those things that nobody was really sure what they were, but looked too important to throw out.

The crucial thing about this box was that it had a small padlock. It also had a very old and tattered sticker of a kitten wearing an eyepatch, which Jelly knew was one of those stickers that would be there for ever.

She tipped the contents of the box – a broken zip and a takeaway menu from the Chinese restaurant that had closed last year – into the bin and gave the insides a quick wipe with some kitchen roll. Then she gave the Blocka Choca bar a deep, slow sniff. It smelt wonderful. She hesitated for a moment – wishing she could eat it. But no – if she did that, she wouldn't have a science experiment.

Her tablet wobbled as she placed it on top of the microwave and tapped the red button on its video camera.

'Good morning,' she said into the camera. 'My name is Jennifer Wellington and this is my scientific experiment to determine' – Gran said that was a good scientific word – 'whether the Chocopocalypse is real or fake.'

She wrapped the chocolate in a plastic bag and placed it into the metal box, filled the gaps with kitchen roll for added protection, and closed the lid. The padlock with four rotating digits clicked firmly into place and she gave the whole thing a good shake to test its security. Nobody was going to get into that, she thought, not without the secret code.

Her experiment was ready.

Jelly tiptoed out into the garden with the box in one hand and her still-recording tablet in the other. The dewy grass seeped into her fluffy 'bunny feet' slippers, making them much less fluffy and much more soggy. Using her elbow, she awkwardly flipped the latch on the shed door.

Inside, she slid the box on a shelf next to some empty paint tins and a deflated space hopper, and placed a large jar of old curtain rings in front of it to hide it completely. She shut the shed up, but before she went back indoors she stood for a moment, looking at Dad's lovingly-watered weeds.

She couldn't bear the feeling of him being disappointed when he found out they weren't 'proper' flowers. Pulling the last cocoa bean out of her pocket, she poked it into the ground and whispered, 'Here's a chocolatey thing for luck, Dad – hope it helps your weeds grow.'

Feeling relieved that she had at least started her experiment, Jelly now began worrying about the end of it.

Would Gran's chocolate still be there on Sunday?

Jelly was still wallowing in her worries on her journey to school when she almost walked into a small group of people blocking the pavement outside Chox. Were they actually queuing to get in? She could hardly believe that anyone wanted to buy Gari's expensive and horrible chocolate.

More banners and signs filled the window now: 'Last of Chocolate Stock,' Jelly read.

And: 'Once it's Gone – it's Gone!'

And: 'We Buy Your Chocolate – For CASH!'

Then she realized Gari was standing on a little box at the doorway of the shop, talking. That was why he had a crowd. What was he saying? Jelly stopped and listened, curious.

'I look around this town and do you know what I see?' the shop owner cried.

There was a pause.

'People trying to buy Blocka Chocas?' said someone.

'I see people seeking the truth of chocolate,' Gari said, ignoring this. '*Real* chocolate! Not Blocka Chocas, or Wacko Chocs, or Whopper bars—'

People began muttering and shuffling away.

'And as a true descendant of the Ancient Easter Egg Islanders, the Chocolati tribe—' Gari went on.

Now this caught everyone's attention, even Jelly's. There was a quiet 'ooooh' sound and everyone turned back.

'The world of chocolate will come to an end,' he shrieked in a high-pitched warble, flicking his hair. 'It will be tragic. It will be terrible. And it will happen. But ... there is hope.'

More ooohs rippled around the crowd.

'A dreamland of chocolate awaits. It awaits for those who believe. Those who *really* believe. Those who are prepared to *show* that they believe. And those wonderful people ... will be taken.'

'But *how* will we be taken?' asked someone, after another pause.

Gari placed his hands on his heart and lowered his voice. 'You will be taken by a majestic serenity.'

'That's a type of camper van, isn't it?' came another voice.

'No, no!' said Gari, looking cross, trying to drown out a sudden sea of voices:

'But you're not going to fit many people in a camper van!'

'Yeah, you'd need a minibus at least.'

'He's right – you're going to need a proper coach with toilets and stuff.'

'One with a telly!'

'Look, look, you don't understand.' Gari smiled, but Jelly thought it looked painful. 'If you believe, you will be welcomed. The whole of humanity will be welcomed!'

A man next to Jelly shook his head. 'That's a lot of buses.'

'Control your own destiny, my friends,' shouted Gari. 'My chocolate temple, Chox, will provide you with opportunities. Buy my pure Chox chocolate and you will be permitted to enter the chocolate dreamland of my ancestors. And from only twenty pounds a box!'

Jelly couldn't believe that people were falling for this nonsense. She was just about to leave when she looked down and saw a little white insect crawl from the doorway of the shop and right on to her school shoe.

'Eww!' she said, trying to flick it away.

Everyone turned and looked at her, including Gari, whose dark eyes narrowed as he recognized Jelly.

'There are those,' he spat, pointing at her, 'who don't understand what purity means—'

'I wouldn't buy anything from this shop,' interrupted Jelly bravely. 'The chocolate's horrible and there are these insects flying around inside too!'

With cries of horror, the crowd melted away and Gari's moustache started twitching furiously.

That'll teach you for being so rude, thought Jelly, and she continued on to school.

At the end of the road she glanced back to see that Gari was left with no customers at all. But a few had gathered around Sir Walter Waffle's statue instead, and were taking turns to lick the lucky chocolate block.

'Gross!' muttered Jelly.

Bogie the homeless man and his scruffy dog were sitting on a big square of cardboard outside the school gates. It was their usual spot. Some children laughed at him as they went into school, which Jelly hated. She felt she should apologize for their behaviour.

'Any spare change, Twinkle?' Bogie asked, as he always did.

Jelly rummaged in a pocket, wondering if she had anything at all. Finding the coins Mum had given her to buy an apple from the school's 'Five-a-Day' stall (which she never did), she dropped them into his paper cup. She always tried to find something for Bogie, and hoped he'd use some of the money to buy treats for his poor dog, who never seemed to wag his tail.

In the schoolyard, everyone was eating chocolate. Everyone. Even Mr Canny the caretaker had a bar of chocolate sticking out of his mouth while he swept up the mass of empty wrappers littering the ground.

'It's like proper crazy, isn't it, Jell,' said Maya, who appeared with a bar of Wacko Choc in her hand. 'I mean, no more chocolate. It's like the end of the world or something.'

'Yeah, proper crazy,' replied Jelly, looking around.

Kids were showing each other the contents of their pockets and lunch boxes – all of it chocolate. Some were swapping bars for other bars. Potsy Potter had his rucksack open at his feet, full to the brim with chocolate which he was selling to other kids.

'I've got sixty-seven hits on my science experiment video already,' said Summer Harris-Tweedy as she swaggered past with her group of giggling goons, 'and I only posted it last night.'

It pained Jelly that she had been one of Summer's hits. It was, in fairness, a brilliant film, but everyone knew her mum and dad had done it for her, like they always did. It had been filmed in a proper laboratory with people dressed as scientists rushing around carrying out crazy experiments, with bubbling beakers of coloured liquids releasing clouds of gas and bolts of electricity whizzing between metal spheres on spikes. It had music and special effects and everything!

'Yeah,' said Maya, 'but you probably watched it yourself that many times.'

Summer smiled angelically. 'It has fifty-six "likes", and everyone knows that you can only "like" something once. How many have *you* got, Smelly?' she asked, pretending to waft away some bad smell.

'I haven't posted mine yet,' said Jelly, but Summer had already waltzed off to annoy someone else.

'I've got four views and three "likes",' said Maya, 'Two of the views are mine and one is my mum's.' Even though she was far off Summer's total, she seemed quite pleased.

Jelly smiled. 'The other one is mine. I think it's great. 'I'll watch it again tonight and get you some more views.'

Maya's experiment was of her measuring a sunflower each day to see how much it grew. In a week it had somehow managed to shrink by five centimetres!

Jelly thought back to her own experiment of the chocolate in the tin, and she worried some more. It wasn't exactly exciting – a tin just sitting there in a shed. It would be too embarrassing for words if she got no 'likes'. She might as well tell the whole world she had no friends!

All the talk of chocolate at school soon sent Jelly's taste buds into overdrive. Everyone was either talking about chocolate or eating chocolate. Even the teachers! Even Mrs Spinster, the head teacher!

There was nearly a riot at lunchtime too. The school menu stated that the pudding of the day was 'chocolate brownie in a chocolate sauce', but they were served apple crumble and custard instead. The rumour was that the dinner ladies had scoffed all the chocolate brownies for themselves.

But there was no need to panic, Jelly told herself as she thought about whether she would ever have another Blocka Choca bar. Other people might be panicking but she definitely wasn't.

No, definitely not ... It was all just madness. Wasn't it?

CHAPTER 7

'Do you fancy a little trip to the Fun-Sized Outlet Park?' Jelly asked Gran after school.

The Big Choc Lot's Fun-Sized Outlet Park was a bunch of shops that sold discount chocolate straight from the huge warehouse. 'You planning on spending the last of my pension money on chocolate, are you?' teased Gran.

Jelly nodded and gave her the biggest grin she could.

Gran grabbed her handbag. 'I can't argue with that!' she said.

They whispered a quick 'bye' to Dad, who was

doing the ironing upstairs (whispering to avoid waking Mum), and hurried out the door giggling excitedly.

At the gate a white van screeched to a halt in front of them and out jumped Dodgy Dave, his mobile pressed against an ear. He wore a paint-spattered

polo shirt and a handful of gold chains jangled around his neck.

'Your dad in, Jell?' he asked, without taking his phone from his ear.

Jelly shrugged, closing the door quickly behind her. Gran gave her a funny look, but didn't say anything.

'Where is he, then?' asked Dave.

Another vague shrug.

'Yep, yep, yep ...' said Dave, and it took a moment for Jelly to realize he was talking into his phone. '... no worries, it's all being dealt with ... yep, yep, the choc is all stocked and locked ...'

'Don't suppose you could give us a lift to the Big Choc Lot, Dave?' asked Gran, giving Jelly a wink. She always knew how to get rid of Dave. 'My knee is playing up something rotten!'

Dave slipped his phone into his pocket. 'Only if you tell your dad I was after him, OK? I've got a special job coming up.'

Jelly nodded and sort of shook her head at the same time – so she wasn't really lying – but she knew she would probably 'forget'.

'One of you will have to get in the back, though,'

said Dave.

Gran insisted that Jelly should sit in the front, and disappeared into the back of the van before Jelly could do anything about it.

'What's the postcode for the Choc Lot?' asked Dave, his finger poised over the satnav.

'But I can show you where it is,' said Jelly. It wasn't far at all and was in the centre of town.

'I know where it is, dur-brain,' said Dave, checking his phone and then punching the postcode into the satnav. 'I always use a postcode, even if I know where I'm going.'

Jelly was afraid to ask, but asked anyway, 'Why?'

'Because it gives me a time to beat.'

'Estimated duration of travel,' said the posh voice of the satnav, 'is seven minutes and thirty seconds.'

'I'll do it in three!' Dave hollered, and hit the accelerator hard. 'We have lift-off!'

Jelly frantically tried to click her seat belt in, and Gran banged her head on the roof before managing to wedge herself between the two front seats. They both took a deep breath and braced themselves as Dave shot down Waffle Road West, yanking the steering wheel around like it was an Xbox controller.

'That was a zebra crossing!' shouted Gran, as Dave had swerved around some alarmed pedestrians.

'Nah, I don't do those,' said Dave. 'People in the middle of the road? That's just dangerous!' He took his hands off the steering wheel and rummaged around in his pockets. 'Here, take the wheel, will you, Jell?' he said.

Jelly stared at Dave, but he didn't look like he was joking. She grabbed the steering wheel, not really sure what to do with it, but holding it as tightly as possible.

'There's a roundabout coming!' she cried frantically.

'Well, give it a little turn then, Einstein!' muttered Dave, trying to unwrap a piece of bubblegum. 'It ain't rocket science.'

Jelly jerked the wheel in one direction. The *wrong* direction! Cars screeched out of their way as they hurtled the wrong way round the roundabout, completely confusing everyone including the posh-voiced satnav. In panic, Jelly squeezed her eyes tight shut, her pounding heart only calming slightly when she felt Dave taking hold of the wheel again.

'I like your style, kiddo!' he winked. 'That saved us a few seconds.' He blew a big pink bubble of gum.

'I wish I'd walked,' groaned Gran.

'I wish I'd stayed at home,' whispered Jelly.

The look on Dave's face said he wished he could go even faster.

And he did!

After a couple more minutes of white-knuckle driving, the brakes squealed, the van lurched to a halt and Gran somersaulted over the handbrake and into Jelly's lap with an 'Ouuff!'

'Two minutes and fifty seconds. In your face, technology!' said Dave, punching the air. 'You'll have to get out here,' he said. 'I can't get any closer.'

Jelly gazed up at the huge dome of the Big Choc Lot – protected by huge iron gates and a security guard – and the Fun-Sized Outlet Park next to it. Long queues of cars were trying to get in. It looked even busier than that day when Creamy Claire's Confectionery House had been selling chocolate splatter cakes at 'better than half price'.

Jelly and Gran rolled out of the van, followed by

a few chocolate mini eggs that must have been rolling around under the seat. Reluctantly Jelly returned the mini eggs back into the van and wondered how Dave could have spare chocolate just rattling around.

'I think I've broken me bum,' Gran groaned.

Dave shouted from a half-wound-down window, 'Tell your dad to ring me, OK?'

Jelly gave him a half-hearted thumbs up before the van disappeared in a blast of grey exhaust.

Gran put her hand on Jelly's shoulder and smiled. 'You know,' she said, 'I'm not sure who looks after who in this family. Come on – let's get in there and buy some chocolate!'

'Chompton's gone mad,' Jelly said to herself two hours later. She'd stretched out on her bed to recover from the trip to the Fun-Sized Outlet Park, but her mind was racing. She wasn't even in the mood to try for the next level in Zombie Puppy Dash.

She and Gran had returned with only five Chocolate Walnut Mini Munches. It was a pathetic result for such an ordeal.

Jelly had always hated how rude some people could be when out shopping, but she'd never seen anyone fighting over chocolate before. There was hardly any chocolate left at any of the shops in the Fun-Sized Outlet Park – which was weird as the Big Choc Lot was right next door – and someone had tried to snatch Jelly's Chocolate Walnut Mini Munches out of her hand. She had held tightly on to them, even though she didn't like nutty chocolate that much.

Was chocolate really going to become extinct? Was that even possible?

The whole town depended on chocolate. What would happen to everyone who lived in Chompton, if chocolate disappeared? All those people who worked in the chocolate shops would be out of work. Then they would move away to find other jobs. There would be even less chance of her dad getting another job, and if everyone moved away, no one would shop at Mum's supermarket and that would close down. Then Mum wouldn't have a job either. It was all becoming horribly real, and it made Jelly feel sick inside.

All the what-ifs and the maybes were giving her a headache. Sometimes she thought about things so hard she forgot to breathe or blink.

Maybe, she thought, there was something that could replace the important ingredients of chocolate. She took a big breath and rubbed her dry eyes. Then she typed 'fake chocolate' into her tablet. Up came list upon list of chocolate recipes, facts and even songs about fake chocolate. Jelly flicked through before making the mistake of clicking on a page of images of real Chompton chocolate. Her mouth fell open, and without realizing what she was doing, she licked the screen. Immediately, she felt silly and wiped away the smudge, accidentally clicking on an advert for Chox.

The website was much like the shop, with elegant photos of dark, immaculate chocolate in unwelcoming surroundings. The pictures, like the ones Gari had on his walls in the shop, seemed too perfect to be real. In one, Gari was shaking hands with a man holding a sack brimming with cocoa beans. In another, he was casually leaning against a huge curved rock, surrounded by lush greenery and looking very smug. The writing was all about the 'purity' of chocolate and there were even percentages and graphs.

There was no mention of how good it was to eat, how it made your stomach all creamy and warm.

He's missing the whole point of chocolate! Jelly thought.

Something about the photos niggled her, but then she saw that the website had exactly zero 'likes', which cheered her up and made her forget her niggle altogether.

CHAPTER 8

Mum was applying the finishing touches to her make-up in the living-room mirror, ready for another night shift. 'Can you put the light on in here, please?' she shouted to Dad in the kitchen.

Ever since Dad had been learning about electrics, he'd practised in their own house, leading to many confusing – and probably dangerous – results. The living-room light had to be turned on from the kitchen switch, and the kitchen light from the living room. The hallway switch operated every light in the house – with the exception of the hallway!

'We spent all last night attaching those security

tags on to bars of chocolate,' Mum told Jelly as the light went on. 'People were *fighting* over the chocolate – if they can't buy any they might steal it. What a nightmare. When we ran out of tags, we had to take them off clothes and razor blades. I shudder to think what I'm going to find tonight!'

'I shudder at the thought of ravioli on toast again tonight,' muttered Jelly.

Dad came to the doorway. 'Oi! I heard that,' he said. 'Well, we're not having ravioli on toast, you'll be pleased to hear. Mum's having the last of the toast for her breakfast and we're going to have something a bit more exotic.'

'Oooo!' said Jelly, cheering up. 'I like exotic.'

'We're having ravioli with naan bread,' Dad announced. 'And on your toast,' he said to Mum, 'would you like marmite or jam?'

'Jam?' replied Mum, looking surprised. 'Do we have jam?'

'Er, no,' said Dad. 'I was kind of hoping you were going to say marmite. And as there's no orange juice left, I found some of that melon and watercress cordial in the back of the cupboard. We had it a while back, and I'm sure it was lovely ...' Mum and Jelly's faces scrunched up, telling him that they didn't quite agree. He shrugged. 'Well, it's all there is.'

Mum nodded into the mirror with a sigh as Dad disappeared back into the kitchen. She piled all the bits and pieces into her make-up bag, which was far too small for all the stuff in it, and twirled a little twirl. 'Will I do?' she asked.

'You look beautiful,' smiled Jelly, and got a kiss on the forehead.

Jelly worried about her mum. She did look beautiful, but she also had bags around her eyes.

'Here you go, Princess Welly,' said Dad, handing Jelly a plate of ravioli with naan bread, and Mum her marmite toast.

The toast was cut into dainty diagonal quarters and Jelly's plate was laid out in a way which she wasn't sure was supposed to be a face or a dinosaur.

'Sorry there are no cheese slices left,' he added.

'That's all right, Dad,' said Jelly. 'It looks lovely, thanks.'

They all munched on their breakfast/dinner combinations while swaying along to the familiar *The Seven Show* theme tune.

'Tonight,' grinned Alice, who tonight had obviously put fake tan on her face but completely forgotten her neck – which made her head look like a toffee apple on a stick, 'we'll be going live again to Easter Egg Island to find out more about the controversial Chocopocalpyse. But in the meantime, it's National Sock Day and to celebrate we'd like you to send in pictures of yourselves with your favourite socks.'

Dad wriggled his feet proudly, his big toes poking through his stripy pink socks.

'Don't even think about it,' warned Mum. 'I'm not having your cheesy feet being beamed to all the homes throughout the nation. It's bad enough that they're in this one!'

After photos of lots of socks, Alice introduced a singer called Donny Daydream, who had the twinkliest eyes and more rings on his fingers than Jelly had ever seen. She quickly sent a text to Gran:

Donny Daydream on 7 Show

Gran replied instantaneously:

Oh my giddy aunt!

Seconds later, they heard the front door open

and Gran came puffing into the room.

'Blimey,' laughed Dad, 'you can move sharpish when you need to!'

Gran squeezed between Jelly and Mum, her eyes fixed on the screen.

'Do you wear socks?' Alice was asking Donny.

The singer laughed and pulled up his trouser leg. Gran's eyes widened at the sight of Donny's ankle.

'Oh yeah,' he said, 'even someone as rock 'n' roll as me wears socks. But I never wear the same pair twice.'

Dad almost choked on his melon and watercress cordial. 'That's proper rich, that,' he said.

'What do you do with your old socks?' asked Alice. 'Oh, I know – do you make glove puppets out of them?'

'Er, no,' frowned the singer. 'I give them to charity.'

The studio audience burst into applause, and Jelly wondered if she would be able to get some of Donny's donated socks as a Christmas present for Gran, and maybe some for Dad too – because he obviously needed new ones... badly.

'And now to Easter Egg Island. Hello, Professor,' shouted Alice, as if she was trying to speak directly over the Atlantic. 'We've been asking viewers to send in their questions, and we've had tons. We'll try to fly through them. First one is: On Sunday – will existing chocolate still be here or will that disappear too?'

Professor Fizziwicks, who was now sitting in front of a tent next to the giant egg monument, nodded as if he was thinking deeply. 'My understanding of the inscriptions is that all cacao material, which is the fundamental product in chocolate, will break down,' he said, his tongue flapping about as he grappled with the long words. 'In modern scientific terms, the molecules will degrade in a similar manner to radioactive particles which decay over a precise timeline.'

'That's complete rubbish,' muttered Gran. 'Scientific codswallop.' But she didn't sound sure.

'So this bar will disappear on Sunday?' asked Alice, holding up some chocolate with the brand name taped over.

'It may become some basic particulate matter,' spat the professor, 'like dust or powder or something similar. We do not know exactly how the transformation will occur. But it will not be anything like chocolate at all.'

Jelly picked up her tablet and typed a question to #AskChocProf.

'Here's a question just in from @jellywellington,' said Alice. 'What about the cacao tree – will it still grow?'

Jelly's mouth dropped wide open. Had they really just said her name? She had only just pressed 'send'.

Awesome!

Mum, Dad and Gran oooooooooh'd in unison. 'What an instant world we live in,' Gran said, shaking her head admiringly.

'Apart from Sunday mornings,' said Mum. She didn't work on Saturday nights, so looked forward to her Sunday morning lie-ins.

'And Tuesday afternoons,' added Dad.

'There are only a small number of areas of the world that have the correct conditions for the cacao tree to grow,' the professor explained. 'Usually in parts of South America and Africa – we call it the Chocolate Belt. Over the last few years, these places have suffered very poor harvests indeed. The basic ingredients for chocolate have been dwindling for a while now. Whether that is due to global warming or over-farming – or *something else* – is unknown right now. It seems very unlikely the cacao tree will still grow.' The words 'something else' jumped into Jelly's head and bounced around annoyingly. *What could that 'something else' be?* she wondered.

'And what time will the Chocopocalypse happen here?' Alice asked.

'The inscriptions refer to the first sunlight on the

Ceremony of the Solstice,' spluttered the professor, 'which will happen at 05:09 a.m. on Sunday morning on Easter Egg Island. Your time difference is plus two hours. This means the corresponding time where you are will be 07:09 a.m. on Sunday morning.'

'Oh, my brain's in bits!' said Alice. 'I don't know what to think.' She leant towards Donny. 'Can I have your socks when you've finished with them?'

Donny's cheeks reddened. 'That's a bit weird, don't you think?'

'Yes, of course it is,' chuckled Alice. 'Forget I said that!'

CHAPTER 9

Bogie and his dog were in their usual spot near the school gates the next morning.

'Any spare chocolate, Twinkle?' he asked Jelly as she approached.

Jelly had been searching for a coin to throw in his cup, and this made her stop dead. Chocolate, not money? She did have the last of the Chocolate Walnut Mini Munches in her bag, and really, she hated nutty things. *But it's still chocolate*, she thought. Two sets of pleading eyes were fixed on her. It was torture! But it was the dog's tail that saddened her the most. The tail that never wagged.

Reluctantly she reached into her bag and handed over her last Mini Munch, getting a whoop of delight and a sharp bark as a thank you. As she turned to head into school, she wondered if she'd even seen the dog's tail twitch.

Her class was even more chaotic than usual. Nobody was interested in Mr Tatterly's numeracy lesson – they were all flitting around talking about chocolate. It reminded Jelly of that time when a Year Eleven kid called Big Craig couldn't stop throwing up on the teachers' table in the canteen. Everyone had raced around in a mixture of confused delight and sheer panic.

Potsy Potter leant between Jelly and Maya, licking his chocolatey lips. 'I've been eating so much chocolate I've even got chocolate-coloured poo!' he said.

'Yewh,' snorted Maya. 'Overshare dot com!'

Jelly was about to point out the obvious when Mrs Spinster, the head teacher, appeared in the room.

'I have a message for the class, Mr Tatterly.'

Mr Tatterly quickly removed his feet from the desk.

'Due to recent events,' continued Mrs Spinster, 'and the insane madness that has infected the world, I have an announcement ...' She paused dramatically.

What on earth was she going to say? Jelly thought. *Would she ever continue?*

'Tomorrow the school will be closed.'

The class burst into cheers of joy.

Mr Tatterly punched the air and shouted, 'Get in!'

Jelly and Maya hugged each other in delight while Potsy Potter jumped on to the table and burst into an elaborate robot dance routine, which was so surprisingly good that Jelly and Maya joined in too!

COUNTDOWN TO THE CHOCOPOCALYPSE:
1 DAY, 22 HOURS, 27 MINUTES, 17 SECONDS

CHOCOPOCAL-APP NEWS

Chocolate factories have been working 24 hours a day to cope with demand. 'It's just like the old days before Health and Safety rules,' said a factory worker called Trevor earlier in the week. 'Everything's running at full throttle. There's a bit of smoke and a funny smell – but it's brilliant!'

However, today the largest chocolate factory in the Great Britain – the Chompton Chocolate Plant – has broken down. Trevor said, 'I've oiled the spigots and greased the bearings of our Large Chocotron Collider, but the poor thing just couldn't take the pace.'

CHAPTER 10

'What a night I had last night!' said Mum, when Jelly got up late the next morning, ready for her day off school. Mum had just come in from work, and she looked exhausted. 'It's like the end of the world. There are security guards on the confectionery aisle now. And they've got those taser things.'

'Taser things?' asked Jelly.

'You know, guns that shoot out wires and give you an electric shock.'

Jelly shook her head. *The world's going bonkers!* she thought.

'Oh yes,' said Mum. 'If you cause any bother on

the confectionery aisle in my shop – you'll be electrocuted!'

'Has anyone been electrocuted yet?'

'Seven people! Including Darren from the fish counter. And he was only trying to break up a fight over a party pack of Chompy Chocs. We've had to close the whole Pick 'n' Mix section down – it was too dangerous!'

Jelly tutted and peered into an empty cupboard for some breakfast.

'I spent hours on the phone and internet trying to find more chocolate for the shop,' Mum continued, 'and there is none! Once the supermarket is empty, that's it. I wouldn't be surprised if I get there tonight and we're not selling any chocolate at all! I'll be quite relieved, to be honest.'

'B-but,' stuttered Jelly, realizing that this wasn't just talk on the telly any more, this was really happening, 'but we have the most chocolate in the world in Chompton. We have the Big Choc Lot!'

Mum nodded. 'Well, none of it's coming to my supermarket, that's for certain. It's like a plague of locusts have gone from one shop to another on a chocolate rampage. Panic-buying! I even heard the hospital is full up with people who've eaten too much chocolate – they're calling it a-lotta-choca-litis.'

She opened and closed various cupboard doors.

'There's probably nothing here either. Yep, it looks like we're out of chocolate. And if what they say is true ... no more chocolate for the Welling-tons, ever.'

She slammed another cupboard door and wrenched open the biscuit tin, shaking her head at a few custard creams and some malt biscuits that nobody liked.

'And there's talk about job cuts happening next week,' she said, clattering the biscuit tin back in the cupboard. 'You can bet your backside I'll be first on that list! Anyway, I'm sick of chocolate. I'm glad it's gone. It was nothing but trouble. We'll all be better off without it. I never want to see another choc-olate thing in my life.'

Dad walked in with a bourbon cream half hanging out of his mouth.

Mum swiped it off him like a tiger.

'What the—?'

Mum threw the biscuit in her mouth, closed her

eyes and chewed frantically, groaning like it was the most wonderful thing in the world. Then she opened her eyes, and went bright red.

'I'm really sorry,' she said. 'I shouldn't have done that. We should have shared it.' Then she turned on Jelly's dad. 'What were you doing with a chocolate biscuit, anyway?'

'I just grabbed a couple to have with my coffee. I didn't realize it was against the law!'

'A couple?' squeaked Jelly.

'You've had the last two chocolate biscuits?' screeched Mum.

He held up another bourbon. 'No, this is the last one!'

This time Jelly snatched it off him. 'We'll do this properly this time, OK! We'll split it three ways.'

'That's not fair,' said Dad. 'Old biscuit-snatcher here has had most of the last one.'

'Yeah, and you had the rest.'

'I'll have half,' said Jelly, 'and you two can have a quarter each.'

'What about your gran?' asked Dad, and got one of Mum's looks.

'Why did you have to bring her into this?' she snapped. 'There's little enough as it is!'

'We'll split it into quarters, OK?' Jelly pulled open a kitchen drawer and grabbed a plastic ruler. She laid the biscuit on a chopping board and used the ruler to measure out quarters, scoring the biscuit with a knife.

Mum and Dad watched with their tongues sticking out.

'It might crumble a bit,' said Jelly, and she sliced through the biscuit with a thud.

Half of it shot straight into the washing-up bowl, which was full of last night's dirty dishwater, and the other half escaped through an open window.

Dad rushed out into the garden. 'It's gone down the drain!' he yelled.

Mum fished around in the washing-up bowl before lifting out the mangled and sodden biscuity remains. 'Anyone want it?' she asked.

Jelly and her dad had shook their heads in disgust, and watched in disbelief as Mum licked the mess off her fingers.

'Morning, all,' said Gran, walking in. 'Look what I found.' She held up half a loaf of bread and a jar of chocolate spread. 'Chocolatey toast, anyone?'

What followed was the best breakfast ever.

When they'd all finished, Mum yawned loud enough to scare a lion.

'I'm off to bed,' she said. 'What you up to today then, munchkin? I hope you're not worrying too much about all of this?'

Jelly shook her head, but Mum kept frowning. 'I know what a worry-pants you are. You should enjoy your day off school.'

'I'm going to check my experiment, then I'm meeting Maya on the High Street,' said Jelly. 'She's getting some new shoes and wants my fashion advice.'

'Ooh, proper girlie shopping, eh,' smiled Mum. 'Can you take Old Bum-stubble with you?' she said, pointing at next door. 'I might actually get some sleep then, without having to listen to her country and western tunes blaring away.'

She left the room and, as her heavy footsteps faded away upstairs, Dad pulled out his wallet. Jelly could see it was empty.

'I'd give you money to get something for yourself if I could ...'

'It's OK, Dad,' whispered Jelly. 'I don't need new shoes, anyway.'

They both looked at her torn and grubby trainers.

'We'll get you some soon, though. Promise,' he said. 'Dave says he's got a special job for me. Can I use your phone for a minute? I need to text him to let him know I'm coming. I don't have any credit on mine.'

Jelly decided to come straight to the point. 'Is Dave's job against the law?'

Dad blinked fast. 'Why do you say that?' he asked.

'Is it against the law?'

He snuggled up beside her. 'Sometimes, grown-ups have to do things we don't always want to do.'

'Is it against the law?' Jelly said again. She wasn't going to put up with her dad speaking to her like a little girl.

'Look,' said Dad quietly, putting his arm around her, 'if I do this job, it'll mean I'll get quite a bit of money. More than usual. And it'll mean that we can get some shopping in. You know, proper shopping. Not just ravioli.' They both chuckled, but Jelly felt tears pricking at her eyes. 'There's a few bills it'll pay off as well.'

'But I don't mind about the ravioli,' Jelly lied.

Dad laughed and kissed her on the head. 'Well, I do. So, can I use your phone or what?'

Jelly shook her head. 'It's out of battery,' she fibbed. She felt terrible about lying. *But telling a lie for a good reason is OK, isn't it?* she told herself. *Or is it still just as bad?*

He gave her another gentle squeeze. 'OK, I'll sort something else out. But I don't want you worrying about stuff like that. We'll be fine.'

Jelly nodded and Dad went back to the kitchen. She froze as her phone beeped, but Dad didn't seem to have heard it.

It was a text from Maya.

I'm @ High St – u gotta get down here. Town's gone mad!!!!

Jelly typed back:

B 10 mins.

In the back garden, Jelly checked her tablet was recording and cleared her throat.

'Day three of my experiment,' she said, squeezing past Dad's weeds and into the junk-packed shed. She focused the camera on to the shelf and moved aside the curtain rings to see the padlocked box with the kitten sticker on it. 'Still nothing to see, but it's early days.' She stopped, wondering what to say next. 'But although there's not much science to report at the moment' – she turned the camera back on to herself, very much aware that this must be the most boring video ever – 'I'd like to add that the world is going properly raving bonkers over chocolate!'

She switched off the tablet and ran back into the house, shouted a 'see-ya-later' and opened the front door just as Dodgy Dave almost fell in.

'Yer dad ready?' he grunted, his phone to his ear and his jaw chomping on bubblegum at the same time.

Jelly stepped outside and closed the door quickly behind her. 'No, sorry, Dave,' she said quietly. 'He's gone out. Gone ... er ... shopping. He'll be ages ... probably.'

'What?' grumbled Dave. 'Well, he's missing a trick.'

Jelly tried her best to usher him down the path before Dad saw or heard him.

'He'll regret it,' Dave shrugged, opening the van door and jumping in. 'Jobs like this don't come along often, you know. He's missing a proper pay-day. Tell him from me – he's a spanner!'

CHAPTER 11

Crowds had taken over the High Street. Cars were being diverted by people in Day-Glo jackets. Jelly couldn't be sure if they were police officers or just people who owned Day-Glo jackets and liked to interfere.

Everyone seemed to be gathering around the town's Chocolate Pole – a stone post decorated with purple flags and ribbons which, it was said, marked the exact centre of the chocolate world. The sun was shining and everyone was wearing brightly coloured summer clothes. But that was where the carnival atmosphere ended. It was more like everyone was waiting for a long-delayed train, Jelly thought, elbowing and muttering to each other. 'Hey there, Jelly-no-mates,' sniped Summer Harris-Tweedy as she and her goons roughly squeezed past. 'One hundred and seventeen "likes" now and rising,' she smirked, but didn't hang around.

Then someone grabbed Jelly's arm and she turned, relieved to see her friend, eyes wide.

'It's exciting, isn't it!' Maya giggled.

'But what's happening? Who's coming?' asked Jelly.

'Dunno,' said Maya. 'Maybe the Queen, or someone from *Strictly*?'

They looked around to catch a view of which celebrity might be appearing.

'Look, there's Mr Tatterly,' Jelly said, catching sight of their teacher. 'I think he's with his wife.'

'That can't be his wife, can it?' said Maya, frowning. 'It might be his dad?'

The screech of a microphone being switched on focused everyone's gaze on to the Chocolate Pole. The girls scrambled up a small wall to get a better view. Jelly's heart sank when she saw a familiar figure in a butterscotch safari suit adjusting a volume control. Gari!

He was now wearing an old-fashioned safari hat and carrying a wooden cane, like some kind of Victorian explorer, Jelly thought. He dabbed his red face with a large purple handkerchief – it was a warm day to be prancing around in fancy dress!

'That's the man from that snobby chocolate shop,' she explained to Maya.

'Oh,' Maya groaned. 'I was really hoping it was going to be the Princess of Pop – Carly Meringue.'

'Good people of Chompton,' shrieked Gari in his weird, garbled accent that was even more ridiculous when he was talking loudly. 'You are at the centre of the chocolate world …'

'Who's the sweaty guy in the stupid hat?' whispered someone in front of Jelly.

'That's old posh-pants from Chox, don't you know,' replied someone else with a lah-di-dah tone.

'Looks like a proper numpty to me,' came another comment, followed by general chuckled agreement.

'. . . and yet your shops are empty of chocolate,'

continued Gari.

Jelly looked around: some people were starting to nod.

'Your children ask you: *Please, Mummy.*' He spoke in a baby voice that made Jelly squirm. *'Please, Mummy, why do you not give me chocolate? Do you not love me any more?'*

The crowd grumbled their agreement and there was no chuckling any more.

'This great town of ours has the biggest choc-

olate warehouse in the world – the Big Choc Lot. Inside is Chompton's chocolate – your chocolate! Yet you go without.'

Angry shouts rang out.

'Today, my friends, you shall claim what you deserve. So together' – he held his cane high, and his voice got louder with every word – 'towards the Big Choc Lot ... WE MARCH!'

With a great roar the crowd moved as one, along the High Street and past Waffle's statue on the corner of Cookie Way and Bittersweet Street. The chocolate block received desperate licks from lots of people, despite the fencing and signs that had been put up around it. Slowly but steadily they moved downhill to the port and on towards the Big Choc Lot itself.

At first, everyone was so tightly packed together Jelly and Maya had no choice but to be taken along.

'Ah well,' said Maya nervously, 'I didn't *really* need new shoes anyway.'

Jelly tried to smile reassuringly but worries flooded her brain. Would they be crushed by a load of sweaty, wobbly people? Should they be doing this? Would the police stop them? What would Gran say? And why was Gari suddenly so keen on ordinary chocolate?

Then thoughts of chocolate, lots of chocolate, took over. The chocolate did belong to the people of Chompton, she thought. Didn't it? It was only fair to share it out.

It wasn't long before they arrived at the huge iron gates of the Big Choc Lot. The security guard, eating a sausage roll in his titchy security cabin, froze at the sight of all the angry people heading in his direction. By now the crowd was punching the air, chanting:

'What do we want?'

'*We want chocolate!*'

'When do we want it?'

'*All the time!*'

With his sausage roll in one hand and a newspaper in the other, the security guard jumped up and ran for his life.

Gari grabbed a huge set of jangling keys from the cabin, and pressed a button to open the gates. The mob flooded through the gap like a herd of wildebeest, and Jelly and Maya squeezed through too, holding desperately on to each other.

At the huge warehouse doors, Gari scrambled on to a stack of crates and held up the keys. 'I take great pleasure,' he shouted, 'in opening these doors for you fine people of Chompton. Inside is everything you deserve.'

Loud and angry cheers rang out. Jelly and Maya hugged each other tightly with a mixture of excitement and jitters, as the doors to the world's largest chocolate warehouse were slowly opened.

As the crowd pushed in, they quietened, as if they were entering some kind of temple. There was a faint but familiar whiff of chocolate, but there were so many people Jelly couldn't see anything – just the large domed roof when she looked up. She was shocked at the size of it. She had seen it from outside, of course, but it looked even bigger from the inside. A bit like the time-travelling Tardis from *Doctor Who*, she thought.

The crowd gradually spread out into the warehouse. Every moment, they became more and more quiet. It was eerie. Something was wrong.

And then Jelly finally realized the problem.

The warehouse was empty.

Not only were there no workers, but there was no chocolate in the Big Choc Lot. None at all!

Jelly raced around, running her hands along the empty shelves and tipping over the few remaining boxes – all empty. Standing on a pile of unused pallets she strained her neck to see as far as possible. But there was nothing: no chocolate and no workers. Had everyone lost their jobs here? *Dad* ... She stopped in shock.

Had Dad lost his job all those months ago because of what was happening to the Big Choc Lot? Was there no more chocolate arriving here in Chompton? How long had this been going on?

'B-but ...' Jelly stuttered at Maya, who was following her, open-mouthed and silent. 'There must be something here. I can smell it.' She took another breath. Either she'd got used to it, or the chocolate smell was disappearing. She looked over to the doors. She could almost see the chocolate smell drifting out of them. 'No!' she yelled. 'Shut the doors! Please!'

Her protests were ignored. Jelly sniffed desperately, again and again and again, sure she could smell the last remaining particles of chocolate being whooshed out into the world.

And then there was nothing left but a dusty emptiness.

Jelly watched as the people of Chompton left the Big Choc Lot. Some were in tears and had to be hugged and comforted. All the protests and anger had gone.

'Not even a single low-fat mini muffin!' wailed one lady.

Jelly noticed a few more of those white insects crawling around the floor. It must be the warm weather bringing them out, she thought, flicking one off her jeans in disgust. She spotted Gari at the doors of the warehouse, surveying the crowd and trying, unsuccessfully, to hide an unpleasant and very smug smile.

After he spoke to someone on his phone he took a large wad of leaflets from an inside pocket of his safari suit and forced them upon the sorrowful crowd.

Maya took one and showed it to Jelly: it was an advert for Chox.

A white van came hurtling through the large open gates to the Big Choc Lot. It squealed to a stop by the warehouse and out jumped Dodgy Dave, who immediately opened up the rear doors. *I bet he had the postcode of the Big Choc Lot already in his satnav and had been waiting for the call*, thought Jelly. Inside the van were boxes and boxes of Chox chocolate.

Gari and Dave seemed to dance among the townsfolk as they waved them all towards the van. Everyone reached for wallets and purses and parted with bundles of cash for tiny boxes of chocolate. Maya unravelled a few notes from her pocket.

'That's for your shoes,' warned Jelly. 'Your mum will go loopy if you spend it on chocolate. And it's not even nice chocolate, believe me.'

'At least there's still some chocolate left somewhere,' Maya said, sounding sadder than Jelly had ever heard her before.

At seven o'clock that evening, Jelly's family sat in the living room, ready to watch *The Seven Show*.

Dad came in with a huge grin. 'I've got some cans of great new fizzy drinks!' he announced.

Fizzy drinks? thought Jelly in delight. It had been ages since they'd had fizzy stuff. Maybe it would make up for the lack of chocolate ...

'I got twenty-four cans for a pound,' Dad said, handing them out, 'and they're only a little out of date.'

'Fizzy *coconut water*?' groaned Gran, looking at the label.

'It's got to be better than melon and watercress cordial,' said Jelly.

Mum read aloud the label as they cracked the cans open. 'Full of electrolytes, it says, and is naturally antibacterial.'

Gran took a swig and suddenly her whole face wrinkled up. 'Are you supposed to drink this or clean the floor with it?'

Jelly wasn't too sure either, but it was fizzy – and that's what mattered. Thankfully, Gran had been to the chip shop, so they all hungrily tucked into a magnificent dinner of chips and ravioli.

'And now we have a special broadcast from Number 10 Downing Street,' said the announcer, 'where the Prime Minister has a message for the nation.'

'What?' moaned Dad with a mouthful of chips. 'What's that numpty want?'

'Shhhh,' whispered Mum, scoffing a toasted chip sandwich. 'It might be serious.'

'Good evening, Great Britain,' said the Prime Minister at a podium outside Number 10. His downturned mouth and stern black suit made him look like he had just come from his own dog's funeral.

'What does it say on that brass plaque on his front door again?' asked Mum. She had helped Jelly with some homework during the Downing Street topic work and had learnt quite a lot – but had obviously forgotten some!

'It says, "First Lord of the Treasury",' reminded Jelly.

'That's right, I remember now.' Mum nodded. 'Because it's weird, isn't it? It should say "Prime Minister" or something like that.'

'It should say "Toffee-Nosed Posh-Boy"!' grunted Dad, who didn't like the Prime Minister.

Jelly smiled in agreement. She had sent loads of

letters to Downing Street asking for her and her class to be able to visit during their topic. They had not received a single reply.

'This proud nation of ours,' continued the Toffee-Nosed Posh-Boy, 'has seen times of strife: the Blitz; penalty shootouts; that very hot day last year when even I had to wear a pair of shorts; and now "the Chocopocalypse" as *The Seven Show* has called it.' He looked awkward for a moment before quickly adding, 'I don't watch it myself, but that's what I am reliably informed.

'In response I demanded a thorough and immediate report. A report written by the greatest brains that were available at very short notice.'

He waved a thick and boring-looking document. The cameras flashed wildly.

'A report which says, and I quote, "There is *probably* nothing to worry about."' He triumphantly slammed down the report and produced his finest politician's smile. 'There, you see. What more evidence do you need? Now let us please, as a nation, return to our normal – and in most cases – very dull little lives. I repeat: there is probably nothing to worry about.'

While he was talking, Jelly noticed a lorry pull up in the background and a man began unloading boxes of 'Premier Chocolate'. Security guards tried to get the man out of shot of the TV cameras. The Prime Minister, oblivious to this, continued:

'But just to show you what a *nice guy* I can be – and this has nothing to do with the election that is coming up – I have ordered a nationwide operation. Tomorrow, every single person in this fine land will receive a Governmental Disaster Chocolate Ration bar in the post.'

'Is this for real?' Gran said.

'Brilliant!' squealed Mum.

'I wish they'd give us a packet of cheese and onion crisps too,' sighed Dad.

'These bars of chocolate,' continued the Prime Minister, 'are coming direct from the nation's ECS – the Emergency Chocolate Stash. Our post office workers, assisted by our mighty military, will be issuing the bars tomorrow in an operation codenamed "Easter Bunny".' A smug grin spread across his face. 'There, you see. I am a *nice guy* after all, regardless of what they say on Twitter.'

A gaggle of reporters tried furiously to ask questions, which the Prime Minister dismissed with a stern shake of the head. He quickly retreated into Number 10.

'Nice guy, my bum,' said Dad. 'He's still not getting my vote.'

CHAPTER 12

The next morning Gran slurped her coffee in the kitchen, while Jelly watched Dad do the dishes and waited to dry them.

'Will the government disaster chocolate be the fancy stuff, do you think?' asked Jelly, thinking back to the horrible chocolate at Chox.

'No way!' answered Dad. 'It'll be bargain-basement cheapo chocolate.'

Gran nodded. 'The fancy stuff will go to the rich and famous. They'll be tucking into it right now, I tell you. And I bet they get more than a bar each.'

'How big do you think the bars will be?' asked Jelly.

'Oh, Jennifer dear, you're driving us mad!' pleaded Gran. 'We'll see this afternoon what we get. I'm sure it'll be lovely.'

'Yeah, there's nothing we can do until the post arrives,' said Dad, looking at the kitchen clock.

'Are you all right Gran?' Jelly asked. 'You sound a bit grumpy.'

Dad snorted, but was ignored.

'Oh, I didn't sleep that well last night,' Gran said, resting her head on her hand. 'Did you not hear all that noise at all?'

Jelly shook her head. She'd got so used to the motorway noise and Mrs Bunstable that nothing seemed to wake her up.

'Police sirens and banging and crashing,' Gran went on. 'I thought for a while they'd finally come to arrest old nosy-bags next door. But it must have been some riots and looting in town. It was on the news. It happened everywhere – the world's going mad. I had to turn my headphones up to "eleven" to block it all out. I've got a stinking headache.'

Jelly's mind turned back to chocolate. Now the

panic-buying had turned into looting, there would definitely be no more chocolate in the shops. Could it really be true that the chocolate she was going to get today was the last bar she would ever have in her life? It didn't make any sense, but it really seemed to be happening. The world had run out of chocolate. No more Blocka Choca bars. Ever! Jelly felt her stomach shrivel in sadness.

The morning drew on. No one wanted to go out or do anything in case they missed the chocolate delivery.

Then, just before midday, Jelly's phone tinkled with a text message. It was from Mum.

I'm coming down. Put kettle on.

Jelly got a mug ready. As she put some coffee in it, the letter box clattered. Dad and Gran froze like statues, and Jelly ran out of the kitchen but was soon back, shaking her head and waving a charity clothes bag, which she slid into the swing bin.

Dad finished some washing up while Gran went back to her magazine.

'What do you think the bars will look like?' asked Jelly.

Gran shot her one of her 'serious looks' and Jelly held her hands up. 'I was only asking!'

Mum came into the kitchen in her dressing gown, her eyes barely open, her face creased.

'What are you doing up?' asked Dad. 'You should be getting your beauty sleep. You need it!' He winked at Jelly.

'Thanks for that, David Beckham!' replied Mum, sitting down and grabbing one of the last disgusting malty biscuits. 'I can't sleep. All I can hear is Bum-stubble slamming her door and ranting to anyone who'll listen.'

Jelly handed Mum her coffee as she swiped through her phone.

'Ooh, Rhona's got her bar,' Mum said. 'Have ours came through yet?' Everyone shook their heads. 'I wonder what they'll look like? Do you think we'll get fancy chocolate?'

Gran rolled her eyes.

'I think they'll have golden wrappers,' said Jelly dreamily.

'Michelle's got hers too. And Donna.' Mum kept scrolling through her phone. 'And Gemma. Are you sure ours haven't come yet? Gemma just lives up the street!'

The letter box clattered again.

'Ha, ha!' laughed Mum. 'Right on cue!'

Jelly ran out, only to see a garish pizza menu on the doormat.

She opened the front door to see Mr Walker was standing patiently outside his house, Truffles squatting by his side, and Mrs Bunstable was in her front garden, pretending to water her hanging baskets but really just nosing about.

'Have you had your chocolate yet, Mrs Bunstable?' Jelly called.

'Oh, you mean the chocolate bars that were on the news?' said Mrs Bunstable. 'Can't say I'm that fussed on chocolate myself.'

Blimey, thought Jelly. She'd never heard of anyone who didn't like chocolate! Especially not in Chompton.

'As long as I can have a custard cream with my cup of tea, I couldn't give a monkey's!' Mrs Bunstable went on, winking. 'Tell you what, love, I'll keep a look out for the postman for you.'

'Thanks,' said Jelly, edging back into the house.

'Oh, you know me,' shouted Mrs Bunstable,

making sure she could be heard by Mr Walker. 'Anything I can do to help. I'm all about helping, me. I do charity stuff all the time. I'll probably get an MBE someday ...'

Jelly glared out of the window, twisting her hair round her fingers. Litter was blowing about in the breeze and she could see a host of burnt-out wheelie bins tipped over in the middle of the road. It was strangely quiet for a Saturday. Maybe everyone was having a long lie-in after a hard night's rioting and looting. Or waiting for their chocolate, just like her? But then, why did so many people have them already? Even Maya had texted to say she had received hers.

What if her family had been missed out? What if their chocolate had been lost in the post?

Dad put the TV on. There was nothing on any channel but footage of the riots. They seemed to have happened all over the world. Cities and towns had been ransacked as people tried to get their hands on any remaining chocolate. When they couldn't, they grabbed anything they could: TVs, games consoles, computers and trainers.

The Prime Minister made another appearance. He announced that after all the problems last night, a curfew would be in place tonight from 6 p.m. No one but the emergency services and the military would be allowed on the streets. Then things got even worse – the TV started showing people with their delivered chocolate bars. They were dancing about, waving the chocolate and the official government letter that came with each bar. Some people were even *eating* the chocolate! Eating it on live TV! Had they no consideration?

Jelly turned the TV off. All she could think about was *her* Disaster Ration bar. It was torture waiting for it. Her tummy twisted and grumbled, but she was saving herself for chocolate. The last chocolate she would ever have ...

After she'd dried up the mugs she went up to her bedroom and lounged in her chair with her feet on the bed. As she did so something suddenly scurried out of one of the turn-ups on her jeans. An insect! Jelly instinctively grabbed a magazine and rolled it up, ready to batter it like Mum would have done.

Then she paused, looking at the insect as it ran across the carpet. Putting the magazine down, she reached instead for a glass and swiftly placed it over the unexpected visitor. She got down on the floor and looked at it carefully. Through the glass, she saw that it seemed to be the same sort of white insect she had seen at Chox. Where had it come from?

Typing 'white insect' into her tablet, Jelly's mind fizzed with questions. After seeing images of loads of freaky insects, she changed her search to 'white insects and chocolate'.

There were even freakier images of insects *inside* chocolate.

'Yuk!' she groaned, then pondered before typing: 'White insects and chocolate crops'.

There were pages and pages of information about cacao trees and bean shortages. Among the many photos of dense green plantations and sacks of beans, one picture caught her attention: a close-up of what looked like a white woodlouse. She clicked on the image.

Jelly read that they were called mealy bugs. There was evidence that they could be responsible for passing on a virus to the cacao tree, which would eventually kill it. They seemed to be partly responsible for the poor chocolate crops of the last few years, and maybe even the Chocopocalypse that was happening right now.

So what were they doing here? In Chox? And the Big Choc Lot? Had Gari accidentally brought some back from his travels? Had they come in a package from one of his tropical suppliers? Now, added to her worries about her free chocolate bar, Jelly's brain raced with even more questions.

She slipped a sheet of paper under the glass and carefully placed the mealy bug outside on her windowsill. It was immediately swept away by a gust of wind.

'Sorry!' she called out, hoping it had landed somewhere safely.

Closing the window, she picked up her tablet and played Zombie Puppy Dash, hoping it would take her mind off chocolate.

It didn't work.

By the end of the afternoon it was obvious: their chocolate was not going to arrive.

The Wellingtons had been forgotten.

Mum went off to bed in a grump. Dad, Jelly and Gran sat in the living room in silence.

At last Gran said, 'Maybe I've got some spare chocolate hidden away. There are so many secret spaces in my Gran-a-van, I'll bet there's a few pieces in a dusty corner somewhere.'

Jelly doubted it, but still smiled at the way her gran kept trying to cheer her up. The mention of a dusty corner, though, made her think of the dusty corner in the shed where her experiment was sitting. She wondered whether she should go out and film another segment. Her final video would have to show different stages of the experiment, but what was the point? There was nothing to film – it was just a boring box!

Worries filled her head. She still had to edit that video and post it online, but she couldn't do that until Sunday when the Chocopocalypse had happened – or hadn't happened. There would hardly be any time for anyone to 'like' it before Mr Tatterly looked at them that night. And it would be a rubbish video that no one would like anyway.

But the thought of that beautiful bar of chocolate just waiting in that box in the shed started to drive her crazy. What if tomorrow she opened the box and it was gone, or turned into – what was it the professor had said ... particulate matter? She would definitely regret not eating it today, when they had the chance.

She made a sudden decision. 'Come on, Dad, come on, Gran,' she said, her stomach churning with both hunger and excitement. 'I've got something to show you!'

Jelly wrenched open the back door and ran out into the garden. The traffic noise had a deeper, booming quality to it than normal – she could feel it inside her chest. Huge camouflaged military trucks streamed along the motorway, heading out of Chompton, their cargos of chocolate delivered. Although, not *all* delivered!

'It was supposed to be my science experiment, Gran,' Jelly shouted over her shoulder. 'But what if I finished the experiment today? Would that be all right?'

'Of course, dear,' said Gran. 'If you think that's best.'

Jelly ran straight to the shed, and reached on to the shelf for the box. If she wasn't going to get any (or many) 'likes', then would it be better not to do the experiment at all? She'd have some explaining to do to Mr Tatterly, but that would be better than being humiliated!

She felt around, pushing the jar of curtain rings away, and pulling down the paint tins and the deflated space hopper.

It wasn't there!

She moved more and more jars, tins and boxes on to the floor. Then she looked on the other shelves, where she knew she hadn't put it – but just to be sure. Where was the box? It didn't make any sense.

She heard Dad calling from outside, over the din of the motorway, 'You all right in there?'

'It's not here!' she yelled. 'It's not here! I need it. It's my experiment!'

Dad squeezed in through the door. 'Where did you put it?' he asked.

'Here,' pointed Jelly. 'Right here. I am absolutely sure.' She could barely speak, she was so upset. Her throat was tight and her breathing was shallow. Her hair was in tangles around her fingers.

'Are you sure you put it in there?' asked Gran,

squeezing in too. 'Have you looked under your bed? Or in your wardrobe?'

'I put it in the shed on the shelf. I know I did – I even filmed it, like you said, Gran. It's a metal box, with a sticker of a kitten with an eyepatch on it. It can't just have disappeared!' Jelly tugged on her hair, wrapping it even more around her fingers in frustration.

'Careful, Jennifer dear,' said Gran. 'You'll pull your hair out.'

'Jelly, please!' said Dad, taking her hand and trying to untangle her hair.

'Stop it,' cried Jelly. 'Leave me alone!'

She ran out of the garden, through the hall and out of the front door, slamming it behind her.

CHAPTER 13

Jelly raced down the street, not sure where to go or what to do. Once she was a few streets away, she slowed down. There had to be something she could do. Her chocolate experiment had somehow vanished and the Disaster bar had not been delivered. This was all just plain wrong. Chocolate wasn't supposed to disappear – if the Chocopoacalypse was real – until tomorrow.

But it wasn't tomorrow yet, it was today. And even if chocolate had disappeared, the box it was in wouldn't disappear with it too. It didn't make sense.

Why no delivery either? Everyone else's bar had

been delivered. Why had they been so unlucky? Why couldn't her family just have one little bit of luck for a change? *I have to do something*, she thought. *But what?*

She made her way into town, past the old Scout Hut that was being used as an emergency centre for *a-lotta-choca-litis* sufferers. A dozen or so pasty-faced patients loitered about the entrance, wearing hospital garments that were open down the back, displaying well-above-average-sized bottoms to the world. *Oh dear*, Jelly thought. *Too much chocolate really isn't very good for you ...*

The further she moved into town, the clearer she saw the results of last night's rioting. Shop windows were smashed and glass still covered the pavements. Litter and empty boxes rolled around in the light evening breeze. Some attempts to board over windows and clean up had been made, but it was still a very sorry scene.

The Chocolate Pole was now bent, with a sign hanging off it that read: 'The End of the Chocolate World is Nigh!' Worse than that, lying face down on the ground, surrounded by litter and sprayed with paint, was the bronzed figure of Sir Walter Waffle. His hand, which had proudly held up the world-famous block of chocolate, had been hacked off. It filled Jelly with more sadness than she had thought possible.

In the window of the Post Office were notices:

'We Have No Chocolate Left – Please Do Not Even Ask!'

'We Have No Cheese & Onion Crisps Left Either!'

Jelly went in and headed straight for the counter at the back of the shop. As she rushed through, a blind was pulled down at the counter, and she was greeted with the word 'Closed'.

'No!' cried Jelly, sprinting forward. 'It's an emergency.'

A multi-jewelled hand from the gloom of the Post Office counter partially lifted up the blind. 'Sorry, but we're closed,' said the hand.

'But it's an emergency! Please! Please! Please!'

'The last post has gone, darling,' said the hand.

'I don't need anything posting,' said Jelly quickly. 'But our post didn't arrive today. We didn't get our chocolate bars! I think they must be somewhere

here – could you please have a look? Please? We're the Wellingtons at number twenty-two Waffle Road West.'

'Wait a moment, please,' said the hand before it disappeared.

Jelly bobbed on the spot, staring at the blind, as if she might burn a hole through it so she could see what the hand was doing. Eventually, the hand reappeared and slid a piece of paper through the gap under the counter.

Jelly picked it up. 'What's this?'

'Form F252,' said the hand. 'Claim form for the non-delivery or damage of items in transit.'

'But ...' mumbled Jelly, 'what do I do with it?'

'Fill in the details and post it on Monday. In six to eight weeks you should get a response.'

'What?' cried out Jelly.

'Thank you – we're closed.' The hand waved and then disappeared for the final time.

A moment later the Post Office lights went out completely.

Jelly wanted to scream. But she didn't. Instead, she trudged back outside and slumped on to a bench. She stared at form F252, as huge dollops of tears smacked on to it.

'Are you OK, there?'

Jelly looked up and blinked. Through her tears she could just make out the figure of a soldier in camouflage gear and extremely muddy boots, crouching down before her.

'Not really,' she mumbled.

'What's up?' he asked gently.

Jelly shook her head. She didn't want to continue crying in front of a stranger. She sniffed loudly and rubbed her damp cheeks with the back of her hand.

'No chocolate ...' she spluttered through her tight throat and tears. 'Didn't deliver ... didn't get any ... they ... forgot us.'

'Tell you what, let me check ...' He pulled out a crumpled sheet of paper from a pocket. 'What was your name?' he asked.

'Jennifer,' she sniffed. 'Jennifer ... Wellington.'

'Well, well, well. It just so happens that you're a lucky one. Your name's on my Operation Easter Bunny list of Possible Forgottens.' He reached into his breast pocket and handed her something.

Jelly took it and looked at it through wide, blurry eyes. It was a bar of chocolate. 'Governmental Disaster Chocolate Ration' was emblazoned across its length in simple black writing on a brown paper wrapper, with a silver foil underneath. On the back, in smaller writing, was 'On Her Majesty's Chocolate Service' next to a small black crown emblem. It wasn't anything fancy, but at that moment it looked like the most wonderful thing in the whole world.

'But ... but ...' Jelly looked up, only to see the soldier's boots disappearing into the back of a jeep and then it zoomed away. 'Thank you,' she whispered.

'Look, look!' screamed Jelly, bursting into the living room.

'Where have you been?' shouted Mum. 'You can't just run off like that. We've been sick with worry! And the curfew's just about to begin.'

Jelly held out the bar. Everyone gaped at it with

giant-sized eyes.

'Where did you get that?' asked Dad.

'I got it from a soldier!' said Jelly. 'Honestly, he said I was on his list.'

'You shouldn't take sweets off strange men,' warned Gran.

'I know, I know,' said Jelly, 'but it just kind of happened.'

Everyone crowded around the bar.

'I'm sorry it's not ginger,' said Jelly, moving it towards her gran. 'Happy Birthday for next week ... you know, just in case chocolate disappears, and I did lose your bar.'

Gran's mouth dropped open and beads of tears filled her eyes, making them twinkle. 'That is the most ...' She struggled for the words. 'That is just ... oh, my beautiful girl.' She kissed Jelly on the cheek, covering her in wet tears. Then she straightened up and said, 'No, no. You have it. It was given to you.'

Mum and Dad nodded. 'You enjoy it, munchkin,' Mum said.

Jelly looked down at the bar of chocolate. To her it was worth a lot more than its weight in gold. But she knew it wouldn't taste as good if she ate it by herself.

'No ...' she finally said. 'We'll all share it!'

'I was hoping you were going to say that!' said Dad, then winced as Mum poked him in the stomach. 'Oh, come on ... we were all thinking it!'

 The four of them danced around the living room, laughing and cheering and crying – while being serenaded from next-door by a Kenny Rogers song.

The bar had six segments.

'Right, let's do this properly this time,' said Jelly.

'Yeah, let's not have any dirty-dishwater-flavoured chocolate this time.' Dad grinned at a red-faced Mum.

They decided to snap the bar into four segments and slice the two remaining segments in half. That way they would each have one and a half segments. Gran did this with expert precision using a carving knife, covering the bar with a tea towel to avoid any chocolate projectiles.

Mum raked around in a kitchen drawer, eventually pulling out some paper napkins with a snowflake pattern and a red trim. 'I know it's not Christmas,' she beamed, 'but it's still kind of special!'

One chunk and a half was placed on to each napkin and handed out.

'Happy Christmas!' said Dad.

'Don't do it!' barked Jelly.

'Don't do what?'

'Singing,' she said, staring at him. 'No singing Christmas songs. I know what you're like.'

'Spoilsport!' he grinned.

They wandered out into the garden to eat their chocolate, but before they could sit down they stopped. Something was strange.

'D'you hear that?' asked Dad, with the biggest smile Jelly had ever seen.

She held her breath. Everything looked exactly the same as usual, but it was also completely different. Then she realized: it was quiet!

Completely and totally quiet. Not the sound of a car, motorbike or lorry. Only a few birds in the distance. Jelly had never heard birds from her house before.

Dad scrambled – with some difficulty – on to the garden recycling wheelie bin and from there on to the flat kitchen roof, showing his family a lot more of his bum than Jelly really wanted to see.

'Put it away,' winced Gran. 'You'll put an old lady off her very last piece of chocolate.'

'What can you see?' asked Jelly.

'Nothing!' said Dad, his arms aloft. 'Absolutely nothing! Come up – you've got to see this!'

'Already with you,' laughed Mum, climbing up the ladder she'd already grabbed from the shed. Jelly watched with a smile as she reached the top and hugged her dad.

'You two have got to come up as well,' Mum called down.

'What?' cried Gran. 'I'll never get up there.'

'Yes you will,' giggled Jelly, pushing her towards the ladder.

After some pulling of arms and pushing of bottom cheeks, Gran was manhandled up the ladder, closely followed by Jelly.

'Do you think this is safe enough?' she worried.

'I'm checking,' Dad said as Jelly reached the roof. He jumped up and down like a crazed monkey on a trampoline.

Jelly, Gran and Mum gripped each other and held on to their chocolate on the napkins – Jelly imagined the whole roof collapsing, taking them crashing through the roof and into the kitchen sink.

'I think it's safe,' said Dad, when no crack appeared.

Mum slapped his shoulder. 'You flaming idiot! Don't do that again.'

'What?' pleaded Dad innocently.

They huddled close to each other, taking in the most wonderful view of an empty and completely silent motorway. All the chocolate had been delivered and no other vehicles were coming to Chompton now – and because of the curfew everyone was at home, just waiting for the Chocopocalypse.

Dad suggested bringing the garden chairs up before they ate their chocolate. It had seemed like a strange idea at first, especially as they were so desperate to tuck into the chocolate, but once they had been roped up and everyone was completely reclined on them, Jelly had to admit that it was the best idea Dad had ever had. He even went back to the kitchen and brought up a cool box full of cans of fizzy coconut water. Mum had her phone with her, but before she had a chance to update her social status online, it ran out of charge.

'Oh well,' she said, putting it away. 'I'll enjoy the blissful silence instead.'

'The soldier who gave you the chocolate, Jelly,' said Gran. 'I mean, who was he? What was his name?'

Jelly shook her head. 'I've no idea. I was just sitting outside the Post Office and he gave it to me.' She didn't want to tell them that she couldn't see him properly because she had been crying so much.

Dad raised his can in a toast: 'To the Unknown Soldier,' he said.

Mum and Gran and Jelly lifted their cans too, before cautiously giving them a sip.

'Geez Louise!' slurped Gran. 'Are we really drinking this?'

'My mouth's gone all squeaky,' giggled Jelly, while Dad rolled his eyes.

'Well, I quite like it,' he said.

Mum smiled at him shaking her head. 'Yeah, you would.'

Their attention then turned to the chocolate.

Should she eat the little bit and leave the big chunk to last so it would last longer? Jelly wondered. Or the big chunk – and then the smaller bit would be like an extra treat at the end ...

'I don't know which chunk to have first!' giggled Gran.

'I was just thinking the same!' laughed Jelly and Mum together. They looked at Dad, chomping furiously on both bits at once with his eyes closed, while wiping his nose with the Christmas napkin.

'Greedy pig!' muttered Mum.

The three of them agreed to have the little piece first as a 'starter' and build up to the main chunk.

'So ...' yawned Dad, 'who's getting up tomorrow morning to see in the Chocopocalypse?'

'What time is it supposed to happen?' asked Jelly.

'Nine minutes past seven,' answered Mum, 'on a Sunday morning. Not a chance!'

They all nodded in agreement.

Dad gulped another mouthful of fizzy coconut

water and let out a satisfied, 'Ahhhhhhhh!' Sitting back in his chair, he lovingly patted his belly. 'I could murder a packet of cheese and onion crisps right now,' he said, but no one was listening. They were each in their own version of chocolate dreamland.

Jelly let the silky smooth chocolate, which was much tastier than the plain wrapping suggested, gently melt and coat the inside of her mouth.

'And no work tonight,' sighed Mum with a smile. 'Isn't that just glorious!'

Once the first piece had completely melted away they simultaneously placed the last remaining chunk of chocolate on to their tongues. Mum snuggled up to Dad, sharing a comfy garden chair, while Gran and Jelly flicked their recliners into a more relaxed shape and drifted off into a chocolatey sea.

'You know,' said Gran, 'if this is to be the end, then I can't think of anyone I'd rather spend it with.'

'Apart from Donny Daydream,' winked Jelly.

'Oh, yes,' laughed Gran. 'Apart from my Donny, obviously!'

They all pointed and giggled at each other's chocolate-covered teeth as the evening sun bathed them in a delicious warmth. Jelly closed her eyes and let the chocolate relax and smooth her senses, then realized something. Whatever happened tomorrow didn't really matter any more.

The thought dawned on her just like the ray of sunshine that glinted from behind the snooker club. Right now – at this very moment – everything was completely brilliant. If she let her worries about tomorrow take over, not just about the end of chocolate, but also about her science experiment and what Gari was really up to, she would miss this moment. And she was determined not to let that happen! Whatever happened tomorrow, they'd deal with it tomorrow.

And even though her experiment had not gone the way she'd wanted, she'd come to a conclusion anyway: Don't worry about tomorrow – enjoy today.

She turned to tell Gran, but stopped when she saw her face. Beautifully illuminated by the sun's golden glow, her eyes were closed and a gentle smile danced across her lips as she sucked on her chocolate.

Mum looked like she might have fallen asleep on Dad's chest, while Dad wrapped his arms delicately around her.

Don't spoil the moment, Jelly thought. Sitting on the kitchen roof, surrounded by complete silence and the people she loved, she wanted this feeling to stay with her and to last for ever. It was perfect. Settling back against the comfy cushions, she closed her eyes and let the last taste of the chocolate disappear from her mouth.

COUNTDOWN TO THE CHOCOPOCALYPSE:

0 DAYS, 08 HOURS, 10 MINUTES, 57 SECONDS

 Chocopocal-App News

Do you love anyone enough to give them your last Rolo?

The Sultan of Swang bought the world's very last Rolo for five billion dollars. He presented it to his wife on a silk cushion during a ceremony at their palace. Unfortunately, as she picked up the precious chocolate, the Sultan snatched it off her and munched it down himself.

Onlookers watched as his wife ran off in tears. A royal attendant said the Sultana was 'not best pleased'.

The two chocolate superpowers, Switzerland and Belgium, are at war. During a Chocolate Crisis meeting the Swiss Chief Chocolatier said: 'Belgian chocolate is not fit for a dead dog.' The Belgian Chief Chocolatier responded with: 'Your chocolate tastes like dirty cheese.' A state of war was immediately declared.

CHAPTER 14

It was agreed that Jelly would sleep in the Gran-a-van that night, much to Jelly's and Gran's delight. Jelly had tried to sleep in the Gran-a-van before, but never managed a whole night. The motorway noise was fine in the day – quite soothing, in fact – but at night it was like trying to sleep in a biscuit tin in a hailstorm. That was why Gran wore her headphones to go to bed, drifting off to 'The Sounds of The Rainforest' or her beloved Donny.

Tonight, there was no need for headphones. It was as silent as ... as ... what? Jelly had never experienced silence like it, so she couldn't compare it with anything! They even opened the windows.

'It's nice to have some company for a change,' said Gran, getting the extra duvet and sheets to make up Jelly's bed on the sofa.

Jelly helped take all Gran's stuff – books, bags and baked beans (baked beans?) – from the sofa to the windowsill, and as she was doing that she noticed Mrs Bunstable on her doorstep.

'What's she doing out at this time of night?' she said, and Gran came to the window.

They waited for their neighbour to go inside her house, but instead Mrs Bunstable did something truly incredible – she stepped off the front step and closed the front door *quietly behind her*. Quietly! No slam.

Gran and Jelly looked at each other in shock. There was something very suspicious going on. Mrs Bunstable *never* shut her door quietly. They watched her tiptoe down the path, clutching her large handbag and glancing furtively around. She pushed the rusty garden gate, which stuck then opened so abruptly she dropped her handbag on the pavement. Jelly and Gran couldn't help chuckling as she tried to pick up the spilt contents, though it was too dark to see what they were. Then off she went up the road.

Jelly stopped chuckling. Now her mind was racing. Why would Mrs Bunstable go out in the middle of the night, during a curfew?

What could be so important?

'Where's she off to, the mad old bag?' asked Gran, echoing her thoughts, but Jelly had already opened the caravan door.

'I'll just take a quick look,' she said.

She quickly crept out to the gate where she trod on something prickly: a big old-fashioned hair curler. It must have fallen out of Mrs Bunstable's handbag. Bending down to pick it up, Jelly noticed a small piece of paper next to it. She held it under the street lamp.

'What?!' she gasped.

'What is it, dear ... *Ow!*' Gran half whispered, half shouted as she stood on the hair curler in her thin slippers.

Jelly waved the paper in Gran's face – she could hardly speak.

'Oh, I can't see that – it's dark, I don't have my specs on and you're shaking it around like a maraca.'

'It's the official letter that came with our chocolate!' said Jelly at last, feeling like her head was about to explode. 'It's got our name and address on it! It must have dropped out of old Bumstubble's handbag.' Then Jelly realized what else had fallen out, but had not been able to see in the dark. 'She's got our chocolate bars! She must have stopped the postman somehow! We have to follow her!'

Gran looked down at her bobbly yellow dressing gown and fluffy slippers. 'But ... but ... I've just got ready for bed,' she spluttered, looking at Jelly who was still wearing her jeans, T-shirt and comfortable trainers. 'I can't just go out like this ... what about the curfew? We might get arrested?'

But Jelly was too cross to think about any of that. 'Come on, Gran!' she said. And before she could think it through, she was out of the gate and running down the street.

'Wait for me!' puffed Gran, running behind her, trying to tie her flapping dressing gown round herself.

Jelly waited for Gran to catch up, and they crept along behind Mrs Bunstable. At the bottom of Waffle Road

West, a flashing blue light lit up the garden walls and hedges – the police were on patrol. Mrs Bunstable hid behind a postbox, and Jelly and Gran ducked down behind a wheelie bin.

'Where do you think she's going?' whispered Jelly as the police car went slowly past.

'It'd better not be far,' moaned Gran, rubbing her feet. 'These slippers are not designed for cross-country running. And neither am I!'

'Couldn't you have found something less ... bright?' Jelly said looking at Gran's almost-luminous yellow dressing gown.

'Oh, excuse me,' snapped Gran. 'If I'd have known I'd be hiding from the police, I'd have worn my camouflage nightie!'

After a minute they saw Mrs Bunstable sidle out from behind the postbox and they followed her to the end of the road and along Cookie Way.

Mrs Bunstable doesn't even like *chocolate!* Jelly fumed. It was only that day she'd heard her say exactly that: 'Can't say I'm that fussed on chocolate myself.' So if she had their chocolate, but didn't like it, what was she going to do with it?

Jelly stopped and grabbed Gran's hand. 'Are you thinking what I'm thinking, Gran?'

'I'm thinking I'm going to have to get some new slippers tomorrow.'

'But I know where she's going.'

'Where's that?'

'Somewhere to make herself some money ...'

Jelly and Gran, kneeling behind a parked white van, watched Mrs Bunstable take out bars of chocolate from her handbag and knock on the door of Chox.

She was going to sell their chocolate to Garibaldi Chocolati!

'That's it!' Furious, Jelly stomped across the

road, Gran hobbling behind. 'That's our chocolate!' she shouted at her neighbour. 'You stole it from us. We waited and waited and waited. While you had them, you greedy—'

'I'm calling the police!' shrieked Mrs Bunstable, making some loose curlers wobble about her head.

'Yes, do that,' said Gran, 'and you can explain to them what you are doing here at this time of night.'

'Well, what are *you* doing here?' demanded Mrs Bunstable.

'Following you!' said Jelly.

There was a clatter as the main door suddenly opened, and out popped Gari's head, looking up and down the street like a spy on a mission.

'I knew it!' Jelly said. 'You're buying stolen chocolate!'

'Ladies, ladies,' he hissed in his strange accent, 'why don't you all come inside and we can talk this through like civilized people.'

Jelly paused at the doorway. The thought of going back into that horrible place made her squirm. But Gran had already followed Mrs Bunstable inside, and Jelly didn't want to be left on the street alone.

There were only few lights on inside Chox, giving the place an eerie feel and it was hard to tell where they were walking.

'Give us back our chocolate,' Gran was demanding.

'I've done nothing wrong,' Mrs Bunstable said. 'You're the ones intimidating an old lady. I'm on tablets, you know.'

'I saw the chocolate ... and you dropped our letter,' Jelly argued, following them past the till and down a corridor.

'This way, ladies,' Gari said behind them, his voice echoing in the darkness.

Jelly was suddenly aware they had moved into a much larger space with a strangely familiar whiff of musty shoes and sweaty socks. She felt a shove from behind and fell forward, stumbling into Gran.

'Ouch!' said Gran.

They turned to see Gari closing some kind of large mesh door behind them and turning a key.

'What's going on?' shouted Gran.

'Where are we?' Jelly said, looking around.

As her eyes adjusted to the darkness, she saw they were in a large area filled with plastic balls and completely surrounded by cushioned black mesh fencing. Around them were soft plastic rectangles, like huge building blocks, and a cushioned spinny-pole thing ... they were in the Barmy Bounce softplay! Even worse, they were in the ball pit!

Mrs Bunstable grinned at them from the other side of the mesh door. 'Ha, that'll teach you! You can't go around following innocent people – that's harassment that is ... Ow! What are you doing?'

'Not too tight, I hope?' said Gari, who had backed Mrs Bunstable up against the spinny pole thing. Using his large purple handkerchief, twisted to form a short rope, her hands had been sharply tied around the pole, making her a prisoner too.

'You can't do this to me,' squawked Mrs Bunstable. 'I'm a senior citizen. I do work for charity ... I've brought you chocolate, just like you said. You told me you'd pay—'

Gari smacked a length of silver tape over her

mouth and gave her a spin. 'That will shut you up, you horrible old woman,' he puffed, dusting down his butterscotch safari suit and taking the chocolate bars from her handbag. He gave them a deep sniff followed by a frown and placed them into several pockets scattered about his safari suit. 'There is a curfew out there, ladies, and I don't need any ... complications.'

He hung the set of jangly keys on to a hook on a central column next to where his safari hat was hanging. There was a panel of switches and a large red button on the column, which Jelly guessed was part of Dad's handiwork and part of the reason the softplay area had closed down.

'Now, what was I doing before I was so rudely interrupted? Ah yes, I was counting the last remaining pieces of chocolate ... in the world!' Gari laughed a laugh that might have sounded evil, if it hadn't sounded so stupid.

'That laugh,' muttered Gran, squinting hard at Gari through the gloom. 'I've heard that laugh before ...'

Gari backed away. 'I don't think so ...' he stuttered.

'I remember!' said Gran, pointing a finger at

him. 'How could anyone forget a laugh like that? You went to the same school as me, didn't you?'

'What?' said Jelly.

'You're the one that would only ever eat chocolate-spread sandwiches for lunch, aren't you?' Gran was laughing now. 'Garibaldi Chocolati, my stars!' she laughed. 'You're Choccy ... Choccy Biccy!'

'Choccy Biccy?' grinned Jelly.

'Don't call me that!' snapped Garibaldi, losing his cool and suddenly sounding very different. 'That is not my name.'

Gran tried to get a better look at him. 'You look different with the moustache and it looks like your spots finally cleared up.' She was enjoying this. 'And didn't you used to be ginger? Is that a wig?'

Everything started to click into place in Jelly's head. The photos on the wall of Chox, the mealy bugs, the shop that no one liked, Gari wanting to buy Mrs Bunstable's stolen chocolate, the photo of him next to the large curved rock – which she now realized was egg-shaped, Dodgy Dave and his special job ...

'It was *you*!' she cried. 'You *started* the

Chocopocalypse!'

Gran turned to Jelly. 'He used to run the school's tuck shop and thought he was the cat's pyjamas ... but the Chocopocalypse? That's a bit much, isn't it, dear?' Her eyes clouded with confusion.

'Indeed, *how* could I possibly do that?' Gari mocked, giving Mrs Bunstable another whirl on the spinny pole, prompting a muffled 'whoop' from the wide-eyed pensioner.

'The white creepy things ...' blurted out Jelly as she tried to sort out her thoughts. 'The mealy bugs. You've been to all the plantations in the Chocolate Belt – I've seen the pho-

tos. You ... you spread the mealy bugs everywhere, knowing that they would kill the chocolate plants.'

'*Why* would I do that? I am a descendant of the Ancient Easter Egg Islanders. I worship chocolate.'

'Because ...' said Jelly, knowing she was right but not quite sure how to explain, 'because you're mad, because you're evil. Because you are only interested in things like *purity*. Chocolate isn't something to *worship* – it's something to *enjoy*. You don't understand chocolate!'

'I don't understand chocolate?' Gari cried out. 'It's *you* who doesn't understand chocolate. You had something pure ... something magnificent. Something worth worshipping. And what did you do with it?' He pointed his cane at Jelly and Gran, as if he was blaming them alone. 'You filled it with bubbles. You put biscuits in it. You mixed it with fruit and nuts. And Chompton was at the heart of this foulness. What were you people thinking?'

The cane pointing continued as Garibaldi Chocolati (Choccy Biccy) bounced towards them on the cushioned flooring like a swordsman fighting an imaginary enemy.

'You gave it soft centres, chewy centres, crunchy centres. You turned it white. You turned it pink. *Pink!* You decorated it. You put sprinkles on it, and swirls and piping. You wrote on it: "Be my Valentine" and "Happy Retirement"! You treated it with disrespect. You don't deserve it. You deserve what you are going to get – a world without chocolate. You had your chance and you failed. My ancestors knew this day was coming. They knew of human greed and the mindless disregard of purity. They foretold it. It was their prophecy.' He stopped outside the ball pit. 'The professor told you!'

'Professor Fizziwicks?' said Gran. 'He's working with you?'

'That old fool?' laughed Gari. '*For* me. I paid him, gave him specific instructions and a map, and it still took him months to find those inscriptions to reveal them to the world.' He chortled. 'All it took was that "chocolate rain" and he was convinced I was right!'

'Because if a chocolate shop owner had discovered the prophecy,' said Jelly, understanding now, 'then nobody would have taken any notice.'

'Exactly, little girl,' said Garibaldi, nodding. 'I needed a scientist. And he was the cheapest. It is my duty ... no ... it is my *privilege* to witness the fulfilment of my ancestors' prophecy. So yes, I ... nobbled the chocolate crops.' He took a small sealed glass tube from his breast pocket. Inside wriggled dozens of tiny white insects.

Jelly flinched. *Yuck*!

'Mealy bugs!' he whispered, holding it up. 'Just a scattering of these little crawly-creepers in the right place can do quite some damage to a delicate cacao tree.' He flicked an escaped bug off his sleeve.

'And that march to the chocolate warehouse,' said Jelly, putting more of the pieces together. 'There were bugs there too. You knew it was empty, didn't you! You were just stirring up trouble and making things worse. You wanted more people to panic about chocolate, making it easier for you to take advantage of them.'

'I didn't put the bugs there,' shrugged Gari. 'They are merely attracted to the cacao scent.' He swiped another mealy bug off his shoulder. 'They get everywhere! But wasn't that wonderful?' he grinned. 'I saw the moment, *the actual moment*, when hope was replaced with bitter reality. I will treasure that moment for as long as I live. And I sold more *pure* chocolate in an hour than I've sold all year!' He spun Mrs Bunstable around on her pole again and she let out another stifled squeak.

'But what now?' asked Gran. 'What about that

posh shop of yours? What's it called ... Socks?'

'Chox!' he snapped back.

'Well, if it's the end of chocolate, then it means no more for you either.'

'But this is my destiny,' Gari said, opening up his arms as if he was about to sing a song in some terrible musical. 'The destiny of my people. To celebrate the end of days. The end of days of impure chocolate. I will take joy in your misery. But until then, in the last few hours, I shall sell the chocolate I have hoarded – and I will become rich!'

'Are you really that ... that ... spiteful?' Jelly whispered.

This terrible man was responsible for the end of chocolate as she knew it, and quite possibly the end of Chompton too.

Gari twirled his moustache and smiled. 'Yes ...' he hissed, as he walked over to the column of switches. 'Yes, I am. And I'll show you ...'

He flicked a switch, which Jelly half expected (or hoped) would electrocute him, if it was anything like the dodgy electrics at home. But instead a whirring mechanical sound started up and a large trapdoor lifted slowly from the floor.

'My chocolate bunker!' he glowered. 'I have been collecting Chompton chocolate for years – and people like Mrs Bunstable have been more than happy to steal their neighbours' governmental disaster chocolate to help me.'

A head suddenly popped up from the bunker.

'Your phone reception down here's a joke, Mr Chipolata,' moaned Dodgy Dave, his phone pressed against his ear, 'I've been trying to order a pizza for hours.'

'It's Mr Chocolati,' sighed Gari, 'and you can't get a takeaway during a curfew, you dimwit.'

Dave tapped the side of his nose, 'Oh, I know people, Mr Chicken-Tikka, I know people.'

Mrs Bunstable let out a grunt that attracted Dave's attention, and then he noticed Jelly and Gran.

'What's with the Spice Girls?' Dodgy Dave asked suspiciously. 'I ain't splitting my share with no one.' He squinted through the darkness. 'All right, Jell? What you doing here? Your dad could've had a share, though, Jell. He missed out big time.'

'Please ignore our ... guests, Mr Dodgy,' reassured Gari, 'and be about your task. Are you nearing completion?'

Dave half nodded. 'I've just about loaded up the van and I've prepped the satnav with our final destination. It says it'll take fifty-five minutes.' He snorted. 'I reckon thirty-five!' He waved a clipboard and retrieved a short pencil from behind his ear. 'It's all going to plan, Mr McSmartie.'

'Well, get to it, my man. We have a very eager buyer ready to part with a choc-a-lot of cash!' laughed Gari. His funny accent was slipping a little, noticed Jelly. Maybe since his secret was out, the pretence wasn't important any more. Gari turned back to Jelly and Gran. 'Tomorrow I will be gone and the town of Chompton will be a chocolate town no more. The end is coming.'

Stepping down into the 'bunker', he disappeared from view, unwrapping and biting into a bar of chocolate as he went.

'You know, Mr Dodgy,' he said, 'these disaster bars aren't too bad!'

Gran gritted her teeth. 'He always was a wrong 'un,' she said.

Jelly nodded. 'The pair of them.'

CHAPTER 15

Jelly felt a dark churning in her stomach. Were there really people as horrible as Gari in this world? She picked up one of the soft plastic balls and threw it with all her might in his direction. It bounced off the mesh and re-joined the thousands more scattered everywhere. The ball would not have done much damage to Gari, even if she could have hit him with it. But it would have been satisfying to have whopped a ball off his head through a gap in the mesh ...

A gap in the mesh!

'Follow me,' Jelly whispered to Gran.

'Follow you?' asked Gran, glancing around. 'Follow you where?'

Jelly dived down and disappeared below the balls, trying to ignore the smell of old, stale, ball-pit balls. And there it was – the hole she'd got through when she was little.

She was a bit bigger now – but she squeezed and wriggled, and soon popped out the other side.

'How did you do that, Houdini?' mouthed Gran.

Jelly pointed down. 'There's a gap!' she mouthed back. 'Come on, Gran. Quick!'

Gran knelt down among the balls. She took a deep breath.

'Why are you holding your breath?' whispered Jelly. 'It's not water, you know!'

Gran shrugged her shoulders, and her ears went

red. She took another deep breath and sank underneath the balls. Jelly watched the balls ripple left and then right, coming towards the mesh and then moving away.

Gran's head poked out at the wrong end of the pit, facing the wrong way. Her glasses were sitting wonkily on the end of her nose.

'What are you doing?' mouthed Jelly.

Gran muttered something back and then swooped back under the balls. Jelly was worried Gran might get spotted, as Dave was going back and forward from the bunker, loading up his van with boxes of chocolate.

Occasionally, Jelly spotted a hand or a bum cheek appearing briefly around the ball pit. Then a foot with a furry slipper shot through the gap, almost kicking Jelly in the face. Jelly grabbed it before it vanished again. There was a muffled squeal.

'Keep still,' whispered Jelly. 'I'm trying to help.'

Finally, she caught hold of the other ankle and pulled with all her might. Gran's nightdress and dressing gown got stuck in the tight mesh gap, revealing enormous frilly pink knickers, but after a lot of huffing and puffing, she finally popped all the way through and sat on the floor, looking like she had just used her yellow dressing gown to parachute out of an aeroplane. She was panting and blinking furiously, and her hair stuck up like she'd been electrocuted.

'You've got really big knickers, Gran,' said Jelly, trying hard to hide a smile.

Gran snapped up her hand. 'That is not a conversation we are having!' She shoved her glasses firmly back on her nose.

There was no time for talking, anyway. They had to get going, and quick, while Gari was busy counting his chocolate. They had to warn someone!

Jelly helped Gran to her feet, and noticed that her dressing gown was now on back to front. Turning in a circle, Gran clearly had noticed too.

'How is that even possible?' she muttered. 'I feel just like that poor man who got stuck in the dodgems.'

Jelly shook her head, then had an idea – actually two ideas.

'Give me your dressing gown, Gran.'

'Give me your dressing gown, Gran … what?'

'*Please*.'

Gran untangled the dressing gown and handed it to Jelly. 'Just because we are escaping from a madman and are facing the extinction of chocolate doesn't mean we can skimp on manners,' she said.

Jelly took the dressing gown and, while Gran was rearranging her nightdress and underwear, she loaded it up with as many plastic balls as she could, tying it up like a bag.

She peeked into the bunker. Gari was still counting every last piece of chocolate, while Dave was trying to hide the fact he was eating it while he was shifting it. If she was going to do this, she had to do it now.

'Wait for me by the front door,' she said to Gran. 'Make sure it's clear to escape. And watch out in case Dave comes out again.'

'What?' asked Gran. 'Where are you going?'

'I'm going to stop him.'

'Well, I'm not going to leave you.'

'Gran ... do you trust me?'

'Oh, of course I trust you, dear, but ...'

Jelly looked deep into her gran's eyes. 'Please ... I know what I'm doing.'

Gran took in Jelly's face, and smiled. 'It's like

looking into a mirror and seeing me when I was your age. You're going to be everything I wanted to be, and more. You can be anything *you* want to be. Go on, then ...'

Crouching to avoid being seen, she hobbled along the corridor linking Barmy Bounce with Chox. Jelly couldn't help but smile – her gran looked like a hobbit who'd just got out of bed.

She grabbed as many foam building blocks as she could and, with the dressing gown full of plastic balls, slowly tiptoed towards Gari ... or Choccy Biccy ... or whatever his name was.

The 'bunker' was the size of a large classroom and filled with metal-framed shelving. It must have held thousands and thousands of bars of chocolate before they had all been removed to be sold in some night-time dodgy deal. Dave was holding a clipboard, making ticks against a list. And Gari was eating another bar of the chocolate he'd said he hated!

The silence was broken by a series of groans, and Jelly turned to see Mrs Bunstable had managed to swivel herself around on the pole and was desperately rolling her eyes and trying to say something.

Was she trying to get Jelly's attention so she'd rescue her? Or trying to warn Gari that Jelly had escaped? Either way, Jelly had to act fast. She dumped the cushioned building blocks where she needed them and climbed. They were spongier than she thought and Jelly wobbled on top, but it was the perfect height for her to hit the 'Emergency Power Off' button.

Which she did with a hard smack.

Instantly, blinding lights of all colours, along with a soundtrack of booming party tunes, illuminated the whole area. Everything jumped into life. The dodgems, video screens, vending machines, slushy machines ... and Mrs Bunstable's spinning pole thing – she was whizzing around like a lost sock in a tumble-dryer. Jelly almost felt sorry for her, but then she remembered their stolen chocolate. And Mrs Bunstable had probably stolen other people's too!

She turned back to the bunker and looked over at Gari, whose chocolate-smothered mouth was wide open in shock. His face was bright red and he was shouting something furiously as he ran to the bunker steps. Dave reached for his phone and frantically tapped it, probably trying to call for some dodgy back-up.

Jelly released the dressing gown. A stream of multi-coloured balls bounced into the bunker, closely followed by the foam building blocks.

When Gari and Dave were covered in a sea of plastic she kicked the 'bunker' doors closed and raced back to the entrance of Chox. That wouldn't hold them for long, she knew, but surely a loud commotion during a curfew would bring the police?

Out on to Bittersweet Street, where she saw Gran crouching behind a small wall and waving. A few bedroom lights were already on in the street, and people were leaning out of their windows. Somewhere she could hear a police siren. The booming bass and flashing light show of Barmy Bounce at this time of night made Jelly feel like an alien spacecraft had crash-landed in Chompton.

Before joining Gran, Jelly noticed the parked white van and recognized it as Dave's. A thought rushed into her head and she tried the driver's door handle, hoping it wasn't locked. It wasn't, so she climbed in. She was only in there, hidden from

Gran's view for a few moments, before she came back out and raced over to crouch behind the wall.

'What did you do inside that place?' asked Gran, beaming. 'It's like Blackpool Illuminations!'

'I saw that Emergency Power Off button that Dad said he had fitted,' said Jelly. 'And knowing that Dad gets his wiring mixed up all the time, I thought it might work as an Emergency Power *On* switch.' She grinned at Gran. 'I wasn't totally sure it'd work, but I thought it was worth a try!'

'I like your logic,' nodded Gran. 'Who'd have thought that your dad being so useless would actually turn out to be useful!'

They saw Gari bursting out of his shop. He spun around, glaring in all directions through narrow, angry eyes.

Dave ran out behind him, holding armfuls of chocolate which he threw into the back of his van. He closed the van door, slamming it shut, but was dropping some of the chocolate in his haste.

Just then they were illuminated by a powerful spotlight from above. For one crazy moment Jelly wondered if it was the same aliens that some said had abducted the Ancient Easter Egg Islanders! Or maybe it was the Ancient Islanders themselves, coming to reclaim the last of the world's remaining chocolate! Jelly was relieved (and a little embarrassed) when she realized it was a police helicopter responding to the disturbance.

Gari and Dave ran around aimlessly, trying to outrun the spotlight. The sound of sirens merged with the pulsating beat of the play centre music. That was when Dave decided to take his position in the driver's seat and just make a break for it.

Two police cars screeched around the corner, their flashing lights and sirens adding to the mayhem. Gari dived into the rear of Dave's van, shedding some of its contents as the van sped off at Warp Factor Five, leaving behind a plume of exhaust and a trail of chocolate bars.

The first police car followed Dave's van into the darkness, while the other came to a sliding stop. Armoured police piled out of the car and began fighting over the bars of chocolate that were across the road. Jelly was sure she had never seen officers eat evidence on TV's *Police! Camera! Criminal!*

'And what were you doing in that van after you

came out of that place?' asked Gran as they watched the police scurry around the ground, picking up every last piece of chocolate. 'I thought for a moment you were going to drive off in it!'

Jelly smiled. 'I fiddled with the satnav a bit.'

Gran's eyebrows narrowed. 'What do you mean – *fiddled*?'

'I changed the destination postcode,' said Jelly, not sure whether she should be proud or embarrassed, 'I nearly changed it to our postcode, but I wasn't sure if that would be good.'

'A big delivery of chocolate to the Gran-a-van would have been lovely,' smirked Gran.

'Yeah, but then I thought of the only other postcode I know ... SW1A 2AA.' Gran shook her head, not recognising it, until Jelly revealed, 'I wrote that postcode on loads of letters ... it's Number 10 Downing Street!' They both tried to stop themselves from laughing out loud. 'If they don't get caught by the police on the way,' continued Jelly, 'then they'll definitely be caught when they get *there*.'

Another police car hurtled into the street, so Gran gave Jelly a jerk of the head, indicating it was time for them to slink off. They were out during a curfew and didn't want to risk being caught and locked up, however innocent they were. Gran tried her best to stop the worn-through and grubby slippers from flicking off with every step.

As they turned the corner of their road, Gran pulled out a yellow plastic ball from underneath her nightie.

'Where was that?' asked Jelly.

'You don't want to know!' replied Gran. 'And let me get one thing straight, young lady ...'

'What's that?'

'The next time you fancy a little midnight adventure,' said Gran, 'at least let me put some shoes on first!'

THE CHOCOPOCALYPSE IS HERE!

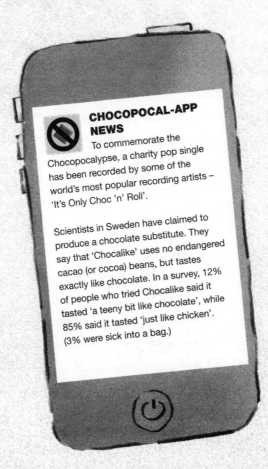

CHOCOPOCAL-APP NEWS

To commemorate the Chocopocalypse, a charity pop single has been recorded by some of the world's most popular recording artists – 'It's Only Choc 'n' Roll'.

Scientists in Sweden have claimed to produce a chocolate substitute. They say that 'Chocalike' uses no endangered cacao (or cocoa) beans, but tastes exactly like chocolate. In a survey, 12% of people who tried Chocalike said it tasted 'a teeny bit like chocolate', while 85% said it tasted 'just like chicken'. (3% were sick into a bag.)

CHAPTER 16

Jelly awoke to the sound of traffic rumbling past and yawned a deep, long yawn. Stretching out her legs, she knocked over some dishes, which clattered to the floor and woke Gran with a jump.

'There's no chicken on Tuesday!' blurted Gran, still half-asleep.

'What?' asked Jelly. 'It's Sunday today, Gran.'

Gran rubbed her eyes, looked around and gave a slightly more sensible, 'Morning, dear.'

The caravan was a mess, since everything had been piled on top of everything else to make room for Jelly's bed on the sofa. Most of it had ended up on the floor.

'Probably best if I make you a coffee in our kitchen, OK, Gran?' Jelly offered.

Gran followed Jelly's gaze, went a bit pink and nodded. 'Give us a minute, to gather myself,' she said.

Jelly pulled open the Gran-a-van door and sniffed at the exhaust fumes. A steady stream of cars was a familiar sight and sound, even on a Sunday morning.

Inside the house, the kitchen was empty – it looked like no one else was up yet. It was only when she saw an empty box of Choco-Flakes squashed flat in the recycling bin that it hit her.

The Chocopocalypse!

Memories of last night rushed into her brain: following Mrs Bunstable and finding out that Garibaldi Chocolati – or Choccy Biccy – had stolen so much of Chompton's chocolate.

Today was the day. The day that chocolate was gone. It was supposed to happen at 07:09 a.m. and it was past 8 a.m. now. Had the ancient prophecy come true, wondered Jelly? The prophecy that Gari had 'given a little nudge'. Had all his hoarded chocolate disappeared too?

And where was he now? Had the police managed to follow and stop him? Or was it too late? She pondered whether she should have done something earlier. She'd been suspicious of him since they had first met. Was it actually all her fault?

Mum wandered into the kitchen, yawning. 'Morning, munchkin, has the world ended?'

'I'm not sure!' replied Jelly.

'I'm sure I'll cope as long as there is a cup of coffee heading my direction,' Mum hinted.

Jelly flicked the kettle's switch to the 'off' position, smiling at Dad's unexpected involvement last night, and got a few mugs from the draining board.

'There's definitely something up,' smiled Mum. 'I wasn't woken up by Old Bum-stubble banging bins and blasting her telly or Kenny bloomin' Rogers for a change. Maybe she's disappeared as well. What a result that would be.'

'Wouldn't that be brilliant!' chuckled Jelly, smiling to herself and wondering if Mrs Bunstable was still tied to that pole? Surely not! She had completely forgotten about her with all the Choccy Biccy goings on. The police had turned up there. They had been going inside. Surely they must have found more chocolate in there? And seen Mrs Bunstable? But they had seemed most interested in the chocolate in the road ... And what had happened to Dodgy Dave and Gari? Had the helicopter caught them? Jelly wondered if she should say something, but decided to explain all later. Gran wouldn't want to miss that!

'I'll put the telly on and see what's what,' said Mum.

The TV next to the microwave oven flicked into life, slowly. The kitchen telly was probably older than Jelly and covered in kitchen grime; Jelly was surprised it worked at all. Mum fumbled with the remote control, pressing all the wrong buttons. Jelly swapped the remote for a steaming mug of coffee and pressed the correct button for the news channel.

A serious-looking reporter in a serious-looking suit wearing a tie with a pattern that would make you dizzy if you looked at it too long was surrounded by captions whizzing around the screen.

There was no sound – her mum must have pressed the mute button. A large red banner read:

Breaking News: Chocopocalypse Now!

Chocolate Crisis: No reported sightings of chocolate

Chocolate Crisis: Belgium and Switzerland Silent

Dad burst into the kitchen, giving both Mum and Jelly a shock. He was wearing a 'Where's Willy Wonka When You Need Him?' T-shirt. 'Has it happened?' he asked.

'Where did you get that?' asked Mum, pointing to the shirt.

'Found it,' said Dad, puffing up his chest. 'On the path outside after the riots.'

'You saw a grubby, stinking T-shirt lying on the ground!' exclaimed Mum. 'And you thought that you would just put it on? And what on earth is *that*?'

Dad looked at the suspicious brown stain near

the hem. 'Chocolate, probably,' he said.

Mum and Jelly watched in horror as he rolled up the T-shirt to give the stain a sniff. Only, he didn't sniff it – he licked it!

'It's not chocolate!' he grimaced.

'I'm married to him, am I?' Mum asked Jelly. 'Please tell me there was a mix-up at the registry office, and Johnny Depp is still waiting for me there, in tears!'

A very weary-looking Gran appeared in the doorway, wearing trainers with her nightie. Her slippers had obviously made it into the bin!

'You off for a run?' Mum laughed.

'Blimey,' said Dad, staring at Gran's wild hair, which she had made no effort to tidy. 'You look like you've been dragged through a hedge backwards.'

'Or a ball pit!' giggled Jelly.

Gran nodded. 'Something like that.'

Jelly handed out mugs of coffee while Mum swiped through her phone and said, 'Michelle's got no chocolate ... Gemma has no chocolate ... Donna has posted a picture of her empty chocolate drawer ...

and Karen has a photo of her cat asleep in the sink.' She showed Dad the picture, and he did a very poor job of looking interested.

'Well, that's that then,' said Gran. 'If Michelle has no chocolate and there's a cat in a sink – it's happened. The Chocopocalypse is upon us!'

Dad picked up the remote and bashed it off the top of the TV. 'I thought I'd fixed this,' he mumbled.

The room was suddenly filled with the booming voice of the TV newsman. 'Chocopocalyptic disaster!' he yelled.

Jelly leant over the microwave and pressed a small button on the bottom of the TV. The sliding volume levels reduced and the newsman stopped shouting.

'No confirmed reports of chocolate have been received, but we have some unconfirmed messages, including a man in Bonnybridge who says he has seen Elvis eating a big Hunk O'Choc bar.'

'Thank you very much!' said Dad with a swivel of his hips – trying to do an Elvis impression but sounding more like a Welshman with a sore throat.

There seemed to be a lot of confusion and nothing much to report. Lots of reporters in various locations repeated the same stuff over and over.

There was no chocolate. Anywhere.

'Well, that's it – I'm just glad it's all over,' said Gran, but everyone looked sad. What would happen to Chompton? What would happen to Mum's job?

Jelly was determined not to let her worries take over again. 'Well, no matter what happens, we'll get by,' she said. 'I mean, it's only chocolate and chocolate was nice, but there's plenty of other stuff.'

'Shortbread,' said Gran.

'Marshmallows,' swooned Mum.

'Oh yeah, marshmallows,' said Dad. 'Dipped in chocolate sauce.'

Mum looked like she was going to throw her mug of coffee at him.

'Jelly beans,' said Jelly.

'Cheese and onion crisps,' said Dad.

They all sighed. Mum went upstairs to get dressed and Dad went outside to water his 'flowers'.

'Any mention of ... you know who?' asked Gran, nodding at the TV.

Jelly shook her head. 'Do you think they got

away?' she asked. 'I mean, not many people could catch Dave the Demon Driver. And maybe they sussed the satnav thing as well and didn't end up in Downing Street.'

'Either way,' reassured Gran, 'they'll not show their faces around this house again. So it's not our problem. But maybe we'll have a word with the police once things have settled down a bit, OK?'

Jelly nodded and then asked, 'But we'll tell Mum and Dad?'

'Oh yes,' said Gran. 'But not just yet. Let's just have a quiet day, eh? I don't have the energy for any more drama!'

Soon Mum came down dressed, her hair in its tight ponytail, and Dad came in holding a bunch of his weeds like they were a fancy bouquet of flowers.

'These are for my favourite wife,' he beamed. 'To cheer you up.'

'Awww,' said Mum. 'They look ... amazing. Thanks.'

He disappeared for a minute, coming back with a large glass vase. They all tried not to smile as Dad carefully arranged the weeds into a limp and spiky arrangement, and stood back to admire his work. 'There you go,' he said proudly. 'You could take a picture and post it to all of your borrowers.'

'Yeah, my *followers*,' nodded Mum. 'I don't have much charge left on my phone, but I'll do that later. Definitely. I'll just ... um ... put the rubbish out first ...' She pulled the bin liner from the swing bin.

'I'll take that out,' said Gran. 'I'm going back in the caravan anyway.' She took the bin bag and wandered off to the end of the pathway. 'That ... oooooh, that woman!' Jelly heard her shout from outside.

She went to the front door and saw Gran glaring into the wheelie bin.

'Why she can't use her own bin, I'll never know,' she continued to mutter, and tried to push the rubbish down to allow some space.

Mr Walker and Truffles were on the grass verge again. 'Things have got worse, poor thing,' he called out when he saw Gran. 'We gave him a bit of that Disaster bar last night. I know we shouldn't have, but we wanted to share it properly ... you know, like a family. And now ... he can't stop pooing. I think we're going to have to get a new sofa!'

'No. You know what?' Gran said, ignoring Mr Walker completely and glaring into Mrs Bunstable's front garden. 'I'll put our rubbish in *your* bin for a change!' She stomped over to the waist-high fence, reached over and flipped open Mrs Bunstable's bin lid. She dumped the bin bag in, making as much noise as she could. 'Let's see how you like *that*!'

Then she froze, the open lid in her hand, staring into Mrs Bunstable's bin.

What is she doing? Jelly wondered.

She watched as Gran pulled their bin bag back *out* of the wheelie bin, and started shouting, 'Jelly, everyone, come and look!'

Mum and Dad rushed to the door.

'Time to call the men in the white coats,' whispered Dad to Jelly as they made their way to the gate.

Gran elbowed Dad in the stomach. 'I heard that. And I've still got all my marbles, thank you – but look!' Gran laughed like a crazy scientist on an old black and white film. 'Look, look!'

They all peered in. Jelly's heart jumped when she saw was at the bottom.

She leant into the deep wheelie bin to reach it,

her feet lifting off the ground as she did. A moment of panic hit her as she felt herself fall, before hands gripped her firmly around her waist and stopped her from going in.

'I don't think your arms are long enough, dear,' laughed Gran. 'I'll see if I can get it.'

Before Mum and Dad could stop her, since she wasn't any taller than Jelly, Gran leant into the bin. Her feet shot straight up into the air and a muffled whoop of surprise came from inside.

Mum, Dad and Jelly tried to get hold of Gran's wiggling legs and not look at the large pink knickers. *Did she have any other colours?* Jelly wondered.

'I'm not sure which bits I'm allowed to grab!' Dad muttered.

Mum was kicked in the face by a trainer and Jelly couldn't stop giggling.

'You're no help!' said Mum, rubbing her nose.

'Try tipping the bin over,' suggested Jelly.

Dad carefully lowered the bin on to one side, and they all pulled Gran out. Finally, she sat on the ground rearranging her dressing gown while fluffing up her hair and panting furiously.

'Oh, my days!' she puffed.

Dad crawled into the bin and came out holding a rusty, bent screwdriver. 'I could use this for something,' he said.

'Oh, for heaven's sake!' muttered Mum. 'If you want something doing ...' She pushed Dad out of the way and climbed into the bin. Seconds later she reappeared, red-faced, her nostrils flaring with disgust. 'Is this it?' she asked, holding out a metal box. On it was a sticker of a kitten with an eyepatch.

'That's it!' shouted Jelly. 'That's my experiment!'

Mrs Bunstable had not only stolen their governmental Disaster chocolate – she'd actually gone into their shed and taken Jelly's experiment too! She must have seen Jelly put it in there – Dad really needed to fix that gap in the fence!

The lock looked like it had been tampered with. It was a little bent and there were lots of scratches around it, which she couldn't remember being there before – Mrs Bunstable had obviously tried hard to get into it. It felt like it still had something inside, but the metal box was quite heavy so it was hard to tell.

'Well, open it then,' said Dad with wide eyes.

'Hold on.' Mum fumbled around in her pocket. 'I'll video it.'

While Mum worked out how to change her camera phone from 'Photo' to 'Video', Jelly placed the box on to the garden wall and wiped the dirt off the top of it. Her heart was pounding and she licked her lips.

'Come on!' said Dad to Mum.

'I think it's recording,' said Mum, not sounding too sure. 'There's a red circle showing.'

'That means it's recording,' confirmed Jelly.

'OK ...' said Gran. '... Action!'

'What do you mean, "Action"?' giggled Dad.

Gran glared at Dad. 'We have to record this in a scientific way.' She looked at Jelly. 'So tell me, what is your name?'

'My name?' asked Jelly, confused. 'Did you bang your head when you fell in the bin?'

Gran put her hands on her hips. 'For the purposes of recording the scientific experiment,' she said sternly.

'Oh,' said Jelly, getting the point. 'My name is Jennifer Wellington.'

'And the date is?'

'It's the Summer Solstice, the twenty-first of June.'

'Has anyone got today's paper or something to prove the date?' They all looked at each other vaguely until Dad pulled out his phone and showed Gran the screen with the date on. Gran held it close to the camera. 'Can you focus on that?'

'Er,' said Mum. 'I don't know how to change the focus. Hang on, it's doing it itself. It's clever this thing, isn't it!'

The camera focused on the phone's screen, confirming the date displayed above the screensaver – a picture of a packet of cheese and onion crisps.

'Most men might have a picture of their wife or daughter on their phone,' said Mum grouchily, 'but not you, oh no!'

Dad shrugged his shoulders and returned the phone back to his pocket.

'And what is this, Jennifer?' continued Gran. 'Explain what you are doing here.'

Jelly cleared her throat. 'Last Tuesday, I put some chocolate into this box. It was an experiment to find out whether the Chocopocalypse was real or fake.' Gran nodded proudly. 'I kept it safe ... or at least I thought it was safe. I locked it using a padlock so no one could open it but me. Now I'll open it ...'

She stopped. Mum, Dad and Gran were all looking at her, waiting.

'Go on, then!' hissed Mum.

'But first,' Jelly said, 'I have to explain that I have already come to a conclusion. And regardless of what is inside the box, my conclusion stays the same. In fact, it doesn't matter what is inside ...'

'Open the bloomin' box!' shouted Mum and Dad together. Gran gave them one of her 'looks', but then gave Jelly a simple nod – it was time to open the box.

Jelly turned the dials on the padlock.

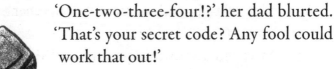

'One-two-three-four!?' her dad blurted. 'That's your secret code? Any fool could work that out!'

'But not Mrs Bunstable,' muttered Gran.

The padlock clicked open and Jelly drew back the lid. Mum moved around to get the camera closer to the inside of the box. With trembling hands, Jelly removed the kitchen roll from the top and sides. She could just see the words 'Blocka Choca' through the plastic bag ...

Jelly pulled the bag from the box. It seemed heavy. Was it chocolate – or was it just the wrapper?

She opened the bag and put her hand inside. Everyone was silent – Jelly wasn't even sure that Mum, Dad and Gran were breathing. She felt a solid lump of something and squeezed it, trying to work out exactly what it was. Then she pulled it out and everyone stepped forward.

In Jelly's fingers was a Blocka Choca bar.

'Is it real?' asked Gran. 'Open it!!'

Jelly ripped open the bar and they all gasped. Inside the wrapper was what looked like delicious, milky-brown Chompton chocolate.

'Eat it! Eat it!' yelled Mum and Dad together.

Jelly broke off a chunk and popped it into her mouth. Instantly a familiar sensation filled her mouth, and her heart beat faster, flooding her brain with pulses of pure joy.

'It's real,' she cried through the mouthful of chocolate. 'It's real chocolate. It really is. It's chocolate!'

CHAPTER 17

The Wellingtons were dancing in the living room when a picture of Jelly and her chocolate appeared on the news.

'We have unconfirmed photographs,' said the newsman, 'of a girl with some chocolate, somewhere in the UK.'

'That's me!' shouted Jelly, staring at the screen in confusion.

'How is that on the news?' asked Gran.

Mum waved her phone in the air. 'I posted some photos online,' she said, 'just a few minutes ago!'

'Oh no,' said Dad, flapping his hands around like

a pigeon. 'Have they got them *all*? Is that picture of me wearing your dress still on there?'

'They're not going to show that on the telly, you idiot,' said Mum. 'Why would they do that?'

'Why is there a picture of Dad wearing your dress?' asked Jelly, as Gran gave her dad a strange look.

Dad shrugged his shoulders innocently. Then the video of Jelly opening the box came on to the TV screen.

'I posted that too,' said Mum, just before her phone rang. She answered it and started nodding, before giving out their address.

'Who was that?' Jelly asked, as Mum clicked the phone off.

'*The Chompton-on-de-Lyte Daily Digest.* They're coming round for an interview and photographs.'

'They're going to interview *me*?' asked Jelly, a little nervously.

'You're the star – of course they're going to interview you,' Dad said. 'If you're OK with that? I mean, you don't have to. We'll all be here with you.'

Gran put her hands to her head. 'My hair!'

Mum looked in the mirror. 'My make-up!'

They both disappeared, leaving Dad and Jelly watching the video. The caption on the screen read:

Breaking News: First Sighting of Chocolate Recorded On Video.

Dad gave Jelly a big hug. 'My little girl, eh!' he said with a giggle. 'On the telly!'

Now it started to sink in for Jelly. She was going to be interviewed! She was going to be famous! Well, in Chompton, at least. She'd better get changed too before the reporter came.

the first sighting of chocolate

She left Dad looking down at his stained 'Willy Wonka' T-shirt and pyjama bottoms. As she ran up the stairs her phone beeped. It was a text from Maya:

Seen the news. U R A Star !!!! X

The next few hours were pure mayhem for the Wellington family. People kept knocking on the door, and beeps and tinkles went off every few seconds on their phones, laptops and tablets – alerts to emails, messages, status updates and notifications. Jelly's video was shown repeatedly on the TV and was being shared all over the world. She felt a mixture of burning excitement and shaky nervousness – she was going viral!

The local reporter came and went, followed by someone from a national newspaper, followed by a lady from a website devoted to chocolate. It was only after Dad had made a cup of tea for someone who had told him he was from the BBC, but was really from the local fried chicken takeaway and just wanted to see the chocolate, that they stopped letting everyone in. Jelly decided to place the few remaining pieces of chocolate back in the metal box for safe keeping. Cars and vans with little satellite dishes on top were blocking the road outside. Film crews and reporters loitered around Waffle Road West.

Some of the reporters had gone into Chompton town centre and were interviewing people for TV. Mum, Dad, Gran and Jelly all watched and pointed out the familiar places in the background. Jelly was particularly overjoyed when she saw her homeless friend Bogie telling a reporter that he knew Jelly and how he was thrilled that the Chocopocalypse had not happened. His dog jumped up and down, trying to bite the microphone – his tail was wagging furiously!

A police officer turned up to stand outside the front door. 'I'm here to keep the situation orderly,' he told Jelly.

'I'm glad you're here,' Mum said. 'It's been crazy! Would you like a tea or coffee?'

'I'd love a strong tea,' said the officer. 'Six sugars please.'

'Six!' shrieked Mum, wondering if they had that much sugar.

'Better make it eight,' he said. 'It's been a

humdinger of a week.'

Mum made him a tea (with only four sugars!) and gave him the mug she had got Dad for his birthday, with the word 'Idiot' on it. He didn't seem to notice.

When Mum's phone beeped a few minutes later, she jumped up from the sofa like she'd been shot out from a cannon as she read the message. 'It's from *The Seven Show*! They want Jelly and Gran on the special edition later! I've got to message them back right now to confirm, then someone will pick the two of you up later and take you to the studio!' she cried.

Jelly couldn't believe it – she was going to be on *The Seven Show*! Sitting on that sofa with Gran, next to Alice! Tonight!

As Gran said right then: '*Oh, my giddy aunt!*'

Two hours later, Mum's phone rang. She stared at the number, then answered the call. She covered over the receiver and excitedly mouthed the words, 'It's *The Seven Show* here!'

Dad squeezed his hands and pulled a face like a little boy needing a wee. Jelly's heart thudded away inside her, like a train speeding down the tracks.

Mum pressed the speakerphone button. 'Your ride to the studios,' said a very posh voice, 'is awaiting the two guests outside your house.'

Mum moved the blinds to one side and looked out. Through the gap, Jelly could see the road was still full of cars and white vans and a gaggle of reporters. They all seemed to be looking up at the roof for some reason.

'Which car is yours?' asked Mum. 'There are loads out the front here.'

'For security reasons you'll have to go to the rear of your property.'

'Oh, OK,' said Mum. 'Give us a minute.'

She kept the phone in her hand while they all made their way to the back. Luckily, Jelly remembered to grab the metal box of chocolate and tuck it into her small purple rucksack. The wind in the garden was terrible. It nearly knocked Gran off her feet and Jelly struggled to keep her hair out of her face, wondering what was going on.

There was an incredible noise, far greater than the normal motorway drone, and it took a moment for Jelly to understand what it was. She looked up and couldn't believe her eyes. A huge helicopter was hovering above their garden! Mum and Dad let out a string of rude words that were drowned out by the mighty machine.

Gran looked horrified. 'I'm not getting in that!' she screamed. 'Not a chance.'

Jelly's mouth dropped wide open. This was her ride to the studios. *Cool as!*

They watched as a man on a winch was lowered into the garden. He landed in the middle of the weeds, and Dad shouted, 'Mind my flowers, will you!'

The man from the sky waved his arms frantically, indicating for them to come forward. Jelly gave her mum and dad a tight, worried hug, and got even tighter and more worried hugs in return. The man wrapped a strap around Jelly and clipped it into place. She realized that Gran was back in the kitchen doorway, shaking her head. Dad ran over, grabbed Gran and flung her over his shoulder while she slapped him furiously on the back with one hand and clung on to her glasses with the other. Jelly couldn't help but giggle, but her mouth was dry and her heart was racing. Dad dumped Gran next to the helicopter man who swung another strap around her. Their feet were suddenly lifted off the ground, Gran's skirt billowing around her head.

'I hope no one is filming this!' she screamed. 'I do

not want my Sunday knickers to be the next internet sensation!'

Jelly and Gran held tightly to each other while they rocked about in the wind.

'Don't worry,' shouted the helicopter man. 'I haven't dropped anyone for ages.'

Jelly made the mistake of looking downwards and saw her mum and dad shrink away as she swayed above the TV aerial. Her stomach lurched. She decided to fix her gaze on Gran, who had her eyes tight shut behind the lenses of her plastic-framed glasses.

At the top, they were pulled into the helicopter by another helmet-clad man and strapped immediately into seats.

Jelly held on tightly to the seat. Her insides were doing somersaults, but the thrill of her adventure meant she was trying hard to stop herself from giggling uncontrollably. The external door slammed shut, instantly stopping the swirling wind. At the same time, the helicopter lurched at an angle and shot into the sky, pushing Jelly and Gran firmly into their seats. Jelly's stomach felt like it had turned inside out!

'Does it have to bob around so much?' asked Gran, looking a little green. She was handed a folded-up bag. 'What's this for?' she asked.

'Vomit,' replied the helicopter man.

'That's nice,' said Gran, 'but I'm sure I'll be OK.'

The helicopter dropped suddenly for a few moments and Jelly felt her eyeballs bulge. Gran promptly opened the bag and stuck her face into it, making gargling noises.

She emerged from the bag, wiped her mouth and whispered, 'Don't tell your mum and dad I was ... you know!'

Jelly shook her head and braced herself for the journey. After all the sudden movements at the start, the ride became much smoother and she quickly began enjoying herself. Out of window she saw that they were way past Chompton and she watched the River de Lyte fade into the distance. It wouldn't take long to get to the TV studios in London, so she wanted to take in every last detail. She had taken the train and underground to the capital plenty of times, but this was something special. It was much better than squeezing on to a carriage full of smelly people in a rush – even if Gran was being sick into a bag!

When the helicopter man told them that they were nearly there, Jelly let out a moan because it was almost over and then a 'oooooh' because of what waited for them. The journey had gone by too quickly.

'You have both used a parachute before, haven't you?' The man grinned.

Jelly's heart stopped. Gran's mouth was nearly as wide open as her eyes.

He chuckled. 'Only joking. We'll be landing on *The Seven Show* roof in five minutes.'

CHAPTER 18

Getting out of the helicopter, they were greeted by a stern-faced man who introduced himself as 'Studio Steve'. Once they'd been ushered, with extreme haste, into the building, Studio Steve told them that they would be going 'live' in twenty minutes and must have a pee before they went on-air. It was a rule.

'Even Donny Daydream had to have a pee!' he said.

Jelly and Gran were herded into the toilets, with Gran tutting furiously, while Studio Steve waited outside.

When they came out he asked, 'Did you actually have a pee or did you just go in there and wait a while?'

'I did.' Jelly nodded. 'I really did.'

He looked at Gran, who hesitated at first ... but then admitted, 'I couldn't. I tried, but I couldn't. I'm too nervous. I really don't need to go.'

'But it's the rules.'

'Oh, for heaven's sake.' Gran went back into the toilets.

Studio Steve and Jelly waited in the corridor, smiling politely at each other.

Gran eventually came out.

'Did you manage a pee this time?' asked Studio Steve.

'Yes!' whispered Gran. 'I did a pee. Honest. Or should I do it in a cup for you to check?'

He didn't answer that, and instead began ushering them down the corridor.

'It's a good job there are no rules on having a poo,' whispered Gran to Jelly, 'otherwise I'd have been there all night.'

They were then plonked on to the studio sofa, with Jelly's rucksack containing the precious chocolate between her ankles. The sofa was not as comfortable as it looked on TV, and the studio itself was smaller than Jelly had imagined. It also had a funny smell. A hot and damp kind of smell – a bit like when Dad did the ironing. Maybe it was a mixture of the blazing lights and sweaty people.

'Can I get you anything?' asked Studio Steve.

Gran shook her head, but Jelly suddenly thought of something. She whispered into Steve's ear, and he shrugged.

'I'll see what I can do,' he said.

Alice and Martin suddenly appeared from behind a load of make-up assistants, and people flapping about with sheets of paper in their hands. They barely seemed to notice their new guests, but then Jelly and Gran were hardly Hollywood stars. Jelly squeezed Gran's hand hard as they heard the show's theme tune and they both started swaying from side to side in time with the music, just as they did at home. They got another look from Studio Steve and stopped, while he counted down from three and then pointed to Alice and Martin.

'Hello!' the presenters said together into the camera, and then waited for the small studio audience (about seven of them!) to stop applauding. Jelly and Gran carried on clapping a little too long, until another look made them stop. 'And welcome to a special edition of *The Seven Show*.'

'Yes, today we are having a *chocolate sundae* ... chocolate *Sunday* ... get it?' chuckled Martin while Alice rolled her eyes. 'We'll be hoping to speak to Professor Fizziwicks later in the show,' he continued, 'for him to explain himself and maybe give a reason for why the Chocopocalypse didn't happen.'

'That's right, Martin,' said Alice. 'And with us here we have internet sensation Jennifer Wellington and her gran.'

My name's being read out on TV! thought Jelly.

'Jennifer, as I'm sure you'll all be aware by now,' continued Alice, 'is the young scientist who conducted a simple experiment—'

'Simple experiments,' interrupted Gran, 'are usually the most important ones.'

'Is that so?' smiled Alice. 'Now tell me, Jennifer, what was your experiment?'

'I just locked some chocolate,' said Jelly, 'into a

safe environment ...'

'Oh, what kind of safe environment?' asked Alice. 'Like a laboratory or something?'

'Erm ... no ... a shed,' said Jelly, then thought she'd better try to make her experiment sound technical. 'I had to isolate the experiment from all possible ... *variables*.' Variables was a good scientific word, she thought.

'I see,' said Martin, shaking his head. 'Shall we just have a look at the video of the first sighting of chocolate after the supposed Chocopocalypse? It has received seven billion hits in just a few hours!'

'Eight billion hits actually, Martin,' said Alice.

'Really,' replied Martin. 'That's incredible! Here's the video.'

The now globally familiar image of Jelly in the front garden came on to the large screen in the studio, and Studio Steve leant in and said, 'And ... off-air.'

Immediately Martin turned to Alice, eyes bulging. 'What do you think you're doing, Alice, correcting me on-air like that?'

'You were wrong. You said seven billion and the autocue' – Alice pointed at the words on the camera – 'clearly says eight billion. It's not my fault you can't read! And you ... old lady person' – Alice pointed now at Gran – 'don't interrupt me, OK?'

Gran nodded, like a little schoolgirl who'd been told off in class.

Studio Steve leant in again. 'Three, two, one ...' He pointed at Martin, who said 'witch' under his breath before producing a huge, wonky smile for the camera.

'Eight billion and one hits now.' He winked at Alice. 'So what was it like when you opened the box?' he asked Jelly.

'W-well, I'd already made my conclusion before I'd opened the box,' answered Jelly, feeling her whole body now shaking with nerves.

'I bet it tasted lovely.' Alice chuckled, but Jelly could tell she wasn't really listening.

Jelly sat up straight, told herself to stop trembling and prepared to tell the world her conclusion.

'My conclusion from the experiment was ...'

'Oh, hang on ...' said Alice, 'we've got to go to some Breaking News ...'

The newsman with the jazzy tie appeared on studio screens announcing, 'In the early hours of this morning a dramatic arrest took place when a van was stopped near the home of the Prime Minister at Downing Street in Central London. After police interviews and further investigations, Garibaldi Chocolati has just been officially charged on suspicion of hoarding and attempting to sell large quantities of chocolate.'

Gran and Jelly gripped each other's hands again. *At last*, thought Jelly. She had started to believe that Gari had got away with his hideous plan.

'Chocolati and his accomplice,' continued the newsman, 'who is believed to be called David Dodgy, were attempting to enter Downing Street with a white van full of chocolate.' The large screens showed an aerial view of Downing Street at night. 'Immediately after their arrest, a quick-thinking police officer loaded the chocolate hoard into a police van and transferred it to St. Ann's Children's Hospital, just around the corner. Aware that the Chocopocalypse was imminent, nurses raced through the wards waking up children to give them – what they believed at the time to be – the last remaining chocolate in the world.'

Gran gave Jelly a light nudge. Her chin quivered and her eyes sparkled. 'You did that,' she whispered. Instead of all that chocolate going to some rich and greedy person, or someone with no idea what chocolate was all about, it had gone to those who would have enjoyed it and loved it the most. Jelly felt good about that – in fact, she felt fantastic!

The TV then showed a reporter standing outside Scotland Yard, where a man wearing a butterscotch safari suit – and handcuffs – was being ushered along by a number of police officers.

'Mr Chocolati,' said the reporter, 'who, as an un-named source has just told us, was previously known as "Choccy Biccy" ...'

'An unknown source eh?' whispered Gran, giving Jelly a wink. 'Who could that be?'

'Don't call me that!' snapped Garibaldi, without a hint of his wobbly accent, as he passed behind the reporter. 'That is not my name!' A blanket was quickly snatched over his head and he was thrown into a police van.

'... is also being connected to problems at Chocolate Belt plantations all over the world, indicating that he may be involved in the chocolate crisis itself.'

Dodgy Dave appeared briefly on screen next, a big bubble of pink bubblegum coming out of his mouth. The thought of both Gari and Dodgy Dave being locked up in something less comfortable than a mesh cage filled Jelly with delight – they deserved it, if they had tried to destroy all the chocolate in the world!

'Well! It's a busy show, isn't it?' Alice said.

Martin turned back to Jelly. 'What did the chocolate taste like, when you opened the box?'

Jelly thought this would be a good opportunity to get the box out of her rucksack, but Alice interrupted, 'Oh, I bet it tasted like honey ... and talking of honey' – she winked at Martin – 'that takes us to our next film.'

'I see what you've done there, Alice. Very good. Just in case the Chocopocalypse did happen, we thought we would come up with some alternatives for those of us with a sweet tooth. Here is Dani Dumper to explain ...'

Studio Steve stepped forward. 'And ... off-air.'

A make-up lady dashed across to dab Alice's forehead while another filed her fingernails. Martin stuffed earphones into his ears and played a game on his phone.

Gran leant towards Alice. 'Do you not ... watch those little films you show ... ?'

'Oh no,' laughed Alice. 'They're usually rubbish. They're just to let the viewers boil the kettle or let the dog out. Nobody watches them, do they?'

'Not really,' agreed Jelly.

Studio Steve stepped back and waved at Martin, who took off his headphones and popped his phone back in his pocket. Alice's make-up ladies retreated.

'Three, two, one ...' said Studio Steve, and pointed at Alice.

'Wow,' said Alice to the camera, 'wasn't that amazing?'

'Yeah,' agreed Martin, reading off the autocue. 'I never knew that about bees.'

'So, Jennifer,' said Alice, 'you were telling us

about your experiment and your conclusion. Well, I would think that the conclusion was pretty obvious, wasn't it?'

'Well,' said Jelly, inching forward on the sofa and clearing her very dry throat, 'the conclusion that I reached was—'

'Oh, sorry to interrupt,' interrupted Martin, putting his finger to his ear, 'but we have Professor Fizziwicks live on Easter Egg Island.'

The large screen in the studio changed to the now familiar backdrop of Easter Egg Island.

'So then, Professor Fizziwicks, the Chocopocalypse didn't happen. Are you a fraud?'

'Oh, my dear child,' said the professor with a chuckle and a spurt of saliva, 'I am no more of a fraud than you. I admit that the date I gave was inaccurate, but it was based on the evidence available at the time.'

'But what about the chocolate rain?' Martin said. 'I was there – I saw it!'

'Ah yes!' spat the professor. 'It is highly likely that the Ancient Easter Egg Islanders built the stone monument over what I have just learnt seems to be a geyser, which squirts up a substance that draws on a reservoir beneath the island that contains years of liquids washed down there from the unharvested cocoa beans that fall from the trees on this special island. Cocoa beans are, of course, the main ingredient of chocolate, so the reservoir produces this wonderful rain at regular intervals – to tie in with the Solstice and the phases of the moon, you see. Very scientific, only something clever people like me would understand, my dear boy. The so-called rain of chocolate therefore neither proves nor disproves the ancient prophecy – and given the timescale of events, any margin of error is incredibly small.'

Martin dropped his mouth open dramatically. 'Incredibly small, Professor? You were wrong! Totally and completely wrong!'

'I was not wrong. Oh no, no, no.' Professor Fizziwicks laughed loudly, his tongue lolling out of his mouth.

'But there are people eating chocolate as we speak! How do you explain that?'

'I do feel a little foolish, I must admit. But I had just slightly misinterpreted the inscriptions. Let me explain ...' The professor took a deep breath. 'This wonderful ancient civilization was based upon chocolate. They celebrated the Summer Solstice like no other. For five days and five nights after the Solstice they would, as the young folk say, party hard. This involved eating lots of chocolate, drinking lots of tropical concoctions, waving their bare bottoms in the air and generally dancing like there was no tomorrow. On the fifth day they would then hold the Ceremony of the Solstice. A much more regal affair with fancy clothes and chanting and so forth. It is the Ceremony of the Solstice that I now believe the inscriptions refer to, and not the Solstice itself.'

'So what are you getting at?' asked Alice, frowning.

'What I'm getting at, my little confused child, is that the date I gave you before was out by a factor of five days.' The professor laughed again. 'Considering we are talking about a timescale of hundreds of years, five days isn't really that much, is it?'

'So you're saying that the Chocopocalypse is still going to happen?'

'Absolutely! This Friday! No doubt whatso-ever!'

People had just got used to the idea that the Chocopocalypse had not happened, Jelly thought, and now they were being told that it was back on! Would anyone believe it this time?

Alice and Martin looked at each other as two police officers, wearing traditional tall blue helmets and not-so-traditional Hawaiian shirts, appeared on-screen behind the professor.

'Come along with us, sir,' said one as he placed his hand on the professor's shoulder. 'We'd like to talk to you about some dodgy money in your bank account and a certain Choccy Biccy ...'

'Oooooh, I like choccy biccies!' said the professor, being escorted away. 'Will there be a nice cup of tea too?'

CHAPTER 19

The show ended in chaos. No one was sure what was happening, so Jelly and Gran made their own exit.

Out in the corridor, people were running about shouting on phones or tapping on tablets.

Jelly said sadly, 'But I didn't get to tell the world my conclusion.'

'I know, dear,' said Gran. 'But if they can't work it out for themselves, then maybe they don't deserve to know.'

'Do you think it would have been better if I hadn't opened that box?' asked Jelly.

Gran shook her head. 'I don't think it would have made any difference.'

'I've reached a new conclusion anyway,' said Jelly with a smile.

'Well, a good scientist should always adapt their theories and conclusions based upon new evidence,' Gran said. 'What is it then?'

'My conclusion is – people are stupid!'

Gran laughed loudly. 'And they prove it *every* day!' She put her arms round Jelly and squeezed. 'Let's get ourselves home, Jennifer dear. I hope you don't mind slumming it on the train with me? I'm not sure my stomach could take another aeronautical assault!'

Jelly looped her arm into Gran's. 'Fine by me,' she grinned. She held up her rucksack. 'I've got the perfect travel snack!'

'Wait there!' came a shout from Studio Steve running towards them. Before they had a chance get away, he caught up to them and forced something into Jelly's hand. 'You asked for these,' he panted. 'It's all kicking off now though, so I've got to go.'

Jelly managed a quick 'thanks' before he ran off and she revealed what she had been given – a pair of Donny Daydream's socks! They both laughed as she handed them to Gran.

'An early birthday present!'

'Oh my days,' said Gran, as she squeezed them against her face and sniffed in deeply, 'they're ... very ... cheesy!'

Back home, Gran and Jelly found Mum and Dad in the garden. Dad was watering his 'flowers', muttering about the wind from the helicopter hurting them, while Mum rearranged flowerpots and blown-over chairs.

'You're back!' called Mum, spotting them. 'You were amazing!'

Dad came over and gave Jelly a hug. 'My very own superstar!'

Jelly noticed that the motorway had gone back to its normal loud drone. *Oh well, it was nice while it lasted*, she thought.

Mum's phone beeped and she pulled it out of her pocket. Her eyes lit up like fairy lights, making Jelly wonder what it could be.

'It's from work,' she said. 'Thanking me for everything I did last week – in an extreme situation, they said – and promoting me to Deputy Assistant Junior Manager!'

'That's brilliant, Mum!' Jelly squeezed her in a hug.

'I'm not a trainee any more,' squealed Mum, spinning on the spot.

'Well done, boss,' said Dad, adding hopefully, 'So that's more money, right?'

Mum beamed. 'Even better, it definitely means no more long night shifts!' She pulled Jelly and Dad and Gran around with her, singing, 'No more night shifts ... no more night shifts!'

She finally stopped and they all steadied themselves on the fence, giggling.

'Mind my flowers!' said Dad.

Jelly stopped laughing suddenly. She stared down at the weeds.

'What's the matter?' asked Mum.

'Dad ...' Jelly whispered. 'Look ...'

Dad bent down to this patch of the garden, and the weeds he'd watered for so long. There, poking out of the brown soil, was a single bright green shoot.

'I put a bean in the ground,' Jelly said. 'One of your cocoa beans ...'

They all peered at the shoot.

'Is that what I think it is?' asked Gran.

Mum leant in and gave Jelly a hug. 'You see, munchkin,' she said. 'Everything is going to be just fab.'

It had been a long day for them all. It had been a

long week! Gran had gone to bed early – she was exhausted. She would be drifting off to sleep to the sounds of Donny Daydream in her ears with Donny Daydream socks on her feet. Mum and Dad were finishing off the last of the fizzy coconut water while they wrote out a long (very long) shopping list. It was Mum's payday tomorrow – and payday always meant Pizza Night! *Double pepperoni pizza with a huge glass of lemonade*, thought Jelly, with her mouth tingling.

In her bedroom, she knelt down by her bed and rummaged around underneath. It was hard to believe that this time last week no one had even heard of the Chocopocalypse! Now it felt like the whole world had changed because of it. Who knew what was going to happen next? Was the Chocopocalypse still going ahead? Well, whatever was going to happen next week, she decided, was going to happen – regardless of whether she worried about it or not.

She found what she was looking for, and slid it out from under her bed. It was an old shoebox.

Making sure her bedroom door was closed, she carefully opened the box. A smile stretched wide across her face.

The box was filled with hundreds of brightly coloured jelly beans.

There's no reason to worry about the future – but it would be silly not to be prepared ...

Chocopocal-App (Version 2.0) News

A global state of emergency has been declared.

Choccy Biccy (aka Garibaldi Chocolati) has been charged with 'Creating a Global Chocolate Catastrophe', which is regarded as one of the most serious crimes there is.

An eighty-five-year-old 'charity worker' has been charged with several Chocolate Related Crimes, which will result in a lengthy prison sentence.

Jennifer Wellington won her school's Science Experiment Competition with 8,301,394,891 views and 794,023,672 'likes'. Summer Harris-Tweedy was in second place with 324 views and 187 'likes'. Maya had 19 views and 14 'likes'. She was delighted.

Cheese and onion crisps stocks are at their lowest levels since records began. The public have been advised not to 'panic buy' and the Prime Minister has announced: 'There is still nothing to worry about, probably.'

COUNTDOWN TO THE
CHOCOPOCALYPSE (RESTARTED): 4 DAYS, 9
HOURS, 38 MINUTES, 11 SECONDS

THE CHOCOPOCALYPSE IS COMING!
(MAYBE?)

WHAT ARE YOU GOING TO DO...?

ACKNOWLEDGEMENTS

Those who made my story real:
To my Chocopocalyptic Champion, Rachel Leyshon. For being my guide, my poker and prodder, and my de-tablizer (still not bitter).

To Barry, for pulling this scribbler and Post-it note hoarder out of your magic author hat, and turning me into a ... well, a scribbler with an even bigger hoard of Post-it notes. Without you, there would be no Chocopocalypse. So it's all your fault!

To Catherine Coe for your essential editorial chocolate sprinkles. Thanks Esther Waller for the copy-edits and pushing my story through the printing processes.

Thank you Lalalimola for your amazingly brilliant illustrations. Your artwork, working with Rachel Hickman, Steve Wells and Kesia Lupo, has brought all those voices in my head to life and therefore proving that I am not (completely) mad.

Thank you Elinor and Jazz for spreading chocopocalyptic panic into the world.

A mahoosive 'sign of the horns' rock salute to the stupidly talented C.J. Skuse. I know what you did ... and I thank you.

I sneaked into Chicken House through their Open Coop and was warmly welcomed by all. I am more grateful than I can express – which is a bad thing for a writer, I know, but I'm still learning.

Those who made my story possible:
A huge cry of 'JellyHeads!!!' to Darren, Craig and Andy. You have suffered decades of my drivel and listened with patience

and humour every time I've uttered, 'I've got a new idea for a book ...'

To all those I worked beside ... well, when I say *worked beside* I should maybe say *sat beside* in various crew-rooms across the world. I learnt the art of never taking anything seriously.

To the Ferrans, for making the good times great, and the bad times better – I owe you more than you know. Friends – in the true sense of the word.

To Philip Pullman, for changing the way I see stories. To David Moorcroft for instilling the sense to never give up. To Frank Turner for being my soundtrack (I hear it even when I'm asleep).

Douglas, Spike, Roald and Sir Arthur – you make my world weird and wonderful, and I love it.

There are two people that I truly owe *everything*:

Thanks Dad – for a head full of stories; thanks Mam – for a life full of love (miss you).

Donna – you have had more faith in me than anyone. For your constant support and encouragement. You told me to write – I doubted you, but did as instructed. Proud to be your husband (... still for ever).

To Trinity ... for being you. You are my reason. I love being your dad.

Those who read my story:

Thank you. I hope my story has been worthy of your time and attention.

And if I've made you smile, then you have made me a happy man.

... and to all you noisy neighbours: Keep it down, eh!

WHO LET THE GODS OUT? by MAZ EVANS

When Elliot wished upon a star, he didn't expect a constellation to crash into his dungheap. Virgo thinks she's perfect. Elliot doesn't. Together they release Thanatos, evil Daemon of Death. Epic fail.

They need the King of the Gods and his noble steed. They get a chubby Zeus and his high horse Pegasus.

Are the Gods really ready to save the world? And is the world really ready for the Gods?

'. . . lashings of adventure, the Olympic gods as you've never seen them before and a wonderfully British sense of humour.'
FIONA NOBLE, THE BOOKSELLER

Paperback, ISBN 978-1-910655-41-2, £6.99 • ebook, ISBN 978-1-910655-64-1, £6.99

THE APPRENTICE WITCH by JAMES NICOL

Arianwyn fails her witch's assessment – instead of qualifying, she's declared an apprentice and sent to remote Lull in disgrace. Then her arch-enemy, mean girl Gimma, arrives on holiday determined to make her life a misery. But as a mysterious darkness begins to haunt her spells, Arianwyn realizes there's much more than her pride at stake . . .

'A charming tale of magic, bravery and friendship, reminiscent of Diana Wynne Jones.'
THE GUARDIAN

'The Apprentice Witch is entirely more charming, adventurous, and full of heart than a book has any right to be. Make no mistake: there's magic afoot.'
TRENTON LEE STEWART, AUTHOR

Paperback, ISBN 978-1-910655-15-3, £6.99 • ebook, ISBN 978-1-910655-62-7, £6.99